The Revenge of the Senior Citizens
**Plus

Also by Kit Reed

The Revenge of the Senior Citizens **Plus

A Short Story Collection

KIT REED

DOUBLEDAY & COMPANY, INC.
GARDEN CITY, NEW YORK
1986

"Final Tribute" was first published in the *Hartford Northeast Current.*
Library of Congress Cataloging-in-Publication Data
Reed, Kit.
The revenge of the senior citizens plus a short story
collection.
On t.p. the word citizens is followed by double
asterisk.
1. Science fiction, American. I. Title.
PS3568.E367R4   1986   813'.54   85–22868
ISBN 0-385-19315-7

For Brian Aldiss with love

Contents

The Revenge of the Senior Citizens
***Plus*

Shan

When Ella Kemper said she was giving another party at her house I thought Oh no, not after the Billie Burke fashion party, where we ended up getting our winter wardrobes for the next ten years because Ella wouldn't let us leave until we did, or the Marvalon cosmetics party, I have enough false eyelashes in my dresser to last ten movie stars a hundred years. Ella gives beautiful parties, but it's always the kind where you have your friends and neighbors in and everybody has to buy something, you know, combining pleasure with profit, like it says in the brochure. As if that isn't enough she won't let you out the door until you've signed up to sell a line yourself, and the clothes or cosmetics or whatever they were always seem so pretty and easy to sell that I end up signing up for a gross of this or a consignment of that because I am convinced that if Ella can do it, I can do it too. Well you just try and invite somebody to your own Tupperware party when Ella has already had hers; they always know your party won't be as good as her party was even if you spend days on the decorations and besides, they've got their own Tupperware to sell.

You would think by this time I would know better, but the thing is Ella's parties are always just lovely, she works on the food and decorations for days and the place always looks just like a fairyland, with angels made out of pie tins and gilded corncobs and at Christmas time she makes gilded macaroni wreaths to hang in the windows; she takes the lids off all her frozen orange juice containers and strings them up on the trees outside, it's the prettiest thing when they all start turning in the wind. But sometimes I do wonder, do you really want all them pastel petty-fours, or the ice cream towers or the violin music like she had for the Farberware party, when every time you take a bite of cookie you know you're going to have to pay?

I would have to admit I always think twice and then I always go, because I don't get invited out that much, being one woman alone, it's a nice change from the television in the mornings and the television in the afternoon and all those times I call my doctor just to hear another human voice. Now my sister Cynthia used to get us out of the house and she would even have people in but she's been gone for five years now, and I would have to admit that if I balanced off the parts I miss, like her company, against the rest of it, I might as well tell you I'm glad I have the morning paper all to myself now, and when I want to go in the bathroom I never have to wait, and I'm glad I don't have to watch her eat toast from the middle out, ever again. Even when I cut off the crusts for her she would start nibbling in the middle, and she would leave the part where I'd gone to all the trouble to cut off the crusts.

So when Ella called I had, you know, mixed emotions, I really do love her parties, but I was standing there in my Billie Burke negligee and the Glamorware mules with the ostrich plumes, I was holding the Tupperware box I keep my stockings in because it was the last of the gross and I couldn't think what else to do with it. I was standing there looking at the plaques and the wastebasket I made out of the découpage kit we bought at that party and I was weighing her invitation, thinking: Can I afford it?

So I said, "I'd love to come, Ella, but can I afford it?"

Well she got huffy and said, "Celia, I don't always have things for sale."

"All right then, what is it?"

"It's a him."

"A man?"

She hemmed and hawed and finally she said, "Sort of. I mean, Celia, all I can tell you is it's a once-in-a-lifetime opportunity, I want you to meet this politician."

"And we're all going to have to campaign and lick envelopes."

"Not exactly." She managed to make it sound important. "He's, well, he's in exile."

"Exile." I was thinking of the Hungarians she had us find homes for all those years ago, the Cubans, the Vietnamese.

"You'll see," she said.

"You're not trying to get us to take in war orphans or anything . . ."

"He's real unusual," she said, and she wouldn't answer another question. "You'll see."

Well I hadn't been out of the house since Alva Edgar's funeral and there was my Billie Burke cocktail gown that I hadn't even worn yet, I told her I'd be there, but at the same time I knew I had better tuck in my checkbook, just in case.

The house looked just like a fairyland, she had sprayed Sara Lee cake tins with red flocking and put them around the doorway so when you came in you knew right away you were somewhere different, and what's more she had put a big orange balloon in the living room ceiling with yellow streamers coming out from it, and all the cookies I saw were frosted in red and yellow and orange and she had even put yellow cellophane around all the lamps so it had a real unearthly glow, and when we were all assembled and a kind of hush had fallen, she said:

"Girls, welcome to the planet Torg."

Now I will go along with anything, I was getting little shivers just like all the rest but at the same time I had this funny feeling, you know, wondering, Is she serious or is she not? Nothing more happened just then, she had pretty drinks of cranberry juice with lemon slices floating in them, I had the idea they might have been spiked so I took it easy, but my they were good. When I asked her about the taste she made me look closely at the ice, would you believe she had put orange juice in shapes and stuck it in her freezer and then put it in the drinks, I told her it was the loveliest thing I had seen in a long time, and she was real pleased. Binnie Osterwald has a grandson that plays one of them Indian things, you know, the sitar, and he was plinking away in the corner while we sat there drinking cranberry surprise underneath that orange balloon, I remember thinking, You know, this really *is* like some other planet, it is hardly like we are in Plainville at all.

By that time we were halfway through the evening and Ella still hadn't brought out any merchandise, those were her Ginny Simms cups and saucers with the delicate shamrock tracery and the silver rim that she's had for years, and her clothes were all things from other parties: the Faith Domergue strapless and the Pantone stockings with the Glintone mules, even the eyelashes were from one of her old consignments, so whatever it was she was selling at this party, it wasn't anything we could see, at least right then, and when I asked her why it was a planet Torg party she said oh, it was just a little old idea she got from the Special Parties issue of *Woman's Day*.

Well I should have known better but I was getting squiffy on the cranberry surprise, I was feeling mellower and mellower, and Ella, she even told us how she made the casserole, you make this bed of Fritos and cover it with Bumble Bee tuna and mandarin orange sections and pour Campbell's chicken soup over that and bake. Of course she made it a little different by grating cheese on top and she put in an egg, like Ella says whenever you ask her any recipe, "I always add an egg," which means she is proving she's better than the directions on any old package, you know, a real cook. The cupcakes were the best, afterward she said she mixed up chocolate Jell-O instant pudding with Duncan Hines cake mix and a couple of other things, and the frosting was really just a light dusting of Jell-O powder, you can imagine how good it was. I was feeling real good by then, happy and sort of special because Ella had never given away *two* of her special recipes in one night, and I was the only one she told. So when she brought him out I thought he was just somebody special to sing or dance to make the party better, like Binnie's cousin, and I thought, Good old Ella, well we deserve it after all those years of buying things.

If I knew then what I know now.

He was young, almost as young as Binnie's grandson, who had disappeared by that time, off to some rock-and-roll concert I suppose. But this wasn't any kid; he was handsomer than anybody I have ever seen, even Eben Ringer, that I almost married when we were seventeen, except that this one had something different about him, his skin was off color just a little, like what was running underneath it wasn't just your ordinary blood, and his head was a little longer than your average, maybe to make room for a special kind of brain. He looked around at us with eyes like electric lamps and when his eyes raked me I thought I was going to die right there, I would of done anything he asked.

"Girls," Ella said, when he had looked around at us and the room was completely silent, "this is a person from another planet," and I tell you, we thought she had gone a little bit too far with her entertainment, but there was not a one of us there that would of denied that's exactly what he was.

Then he spoke, all he said was, "Good evening," but we knew.

After that it turned out the balloon up in the ceiling, that I told you about? Well it wasn't a balloon after all, it was more like a special projector, except the pictures were all inside of it? It was kind of like a crazy crystal ball, and we all sat there with our cranberry juice drinks with the frozen orange juice shapes clinking against the glass while he told us such a story as you would never believe outside a fairy tale, except there were the pictures inside the ball to prove it was true.

It turned out they were pictures of the place he came from, with these fierce good-looking people wandering up and down these buildings he said were all made out of ivory, although I swear to God I never heard tell of elephants that big. The sky was a funny color too, but never mind, if the lights went on and these turned out to be Puppetoons that was still a good show.

Funny thing was it wasn't Puppetoons, he was making those pictures with this thing he took out of his pocket, it was like he shot them into the air and the balloon or whatever it was took them and made them bigger so we could see. We looked at a whole bunch of them ivory houses and then we looked at his house, him with his mother and father, except he called them Mentors, and I thought about having him to bring up and send off to school in the mornings with the lunch pail and the slicked-down hair and I thought, Aaaawww.

The next thing was this picture of a whole bunch of them sitting around in this red garden and then everybody got a scared look because this elephant was coming over the hill, at least I think it was an elephant but it was so big that the only things that would fit in the picture were this big hoof with big yellow nails on it and the tippy end of this enormous tusk and he never spoke or anything but he managed to make it plain that these things were overrunning his world now, there wasn't any place for a body to sit down or build a house because of all the giant elephants and something had to give, either the elephants or them. When we got to see the pictures of the war, it was terrible, by the time it was over they were all retching and staggering around because the air was poisoned and all the plants were poison too, they all had to take canned things into the underground shelters and they only had X years of food and oxygen left.

He raked us with those eyes again, it made you go all weak to see them, and he said, "And so you see, I need your help, you good ladies can be my missionaries, and you will be rewarded in the new civilization."

So I guess it was a little bit like a Tupperware party after all, we were supposed to give parties like this one for all our friends and we would all get to take one of those picture balloons and when we got a bunch together Shan would come and talk to them personally, no obligation and nothing to buy, and we would earn his eternal gratitude. So that sounded good but there was this long silence while we all thought about it, you know, trying to work it out: what he wanted us to do.

Then Ella spoke up, after all it was her party, and she said, "Shan, honey, you'd better tell the girls what it is you need."

He looked at her like she was a damn fool and I thought she was a little bit slow myself, he said, "My dear we need a new place."

"What kind of place?"

"This place," he said, and spread his hands wide enough to take in the entire world.

Now I thought that wasn't such a bad idea, after all, we had opened up our hearts to the Hungarians and the Cubans and the Vietnamese, but then Binnie, it was, had to ask:

"How many of you are there?"

Well the figure was, if you'll pardon the expression, astronomical, and everybody gasped and muttered and finally Ella said,

"Shan, honey, what would we have to do?"

Well it was simple enough, we would give these parties and get fifty people into every one of them, and those fifty would get together another fifty each, and at the end of every party everybody there would be given this beautiful Torg mastodon tusk brooch, set with real emeralds, and all we had to do was wear the brooch, there was one stone that would come out of the center, not spoiling anything, and all you had to do was sneak it into the reservoir?

You can imagine the fuss the girls made, they wanted to know what that would do to the water and Shan, he wouldn't exactly say, he would only say, It makes it good for Torgans too, and besides, as long as you wear your beautiful brooch it won't bother you, and I can tell you that made some people suspicious, Binnie said, Why don't you go to the UN and get a right regular entrance permit, and all Shan would say was, Some times the longest way round is the shortest way home. Then Ella said, You never told us what was going to happen to the water, but Shan, he just smiled that gorgeous smile and said, All of Torg will be grateful to you.

I could see the way things were going, Ella and Binnie were muttering in a corner and the others were all hissing and chattering, you know, agitated, and I thought, Poor Shan, he has come all this way and the girls aren't going to help. Then I caught what one of them was saying and I slipped over to Shan and touched the brooch and I whispered:

"You better look sharp, honey, I think these girls are thinking to turn you in."

Well you should of seen the look he gave me, it would have melted a brick. He sort of aimed the brooch and whispered, "Are you with me?"

So I looked into them eyes and I said, "Yes, Shan, I am."

It only took a second; the brooch he was holding was all it took to do the trick, the beam came right out the point of the tusk. I felt a little bad about it but not for long, because I am Shan's best friend now, and when I looked around and saw the rest of the girls I knew I wouldn't have any competition, no mealy mouths coming around to take him out riding, no prissy faces bringing in covered dishes or brownies or angel cakes that they made from a mix and were trying to pass off as an old family recipe.

What that brooch did was, it beamed out in some weird way that a scientist would have to explain to you, and there were all those girls that I got old with, they weren't hurt a bit but they wouldn't hurt anybody else again either, Ella wouldn't be giving any more parties that it cost you a hundred bucks just to get out the door, and at that you would have to take home a lot of junk you didn't need. Binnie wouldn't be going around to the rock-and-roll concert to bother her grandson and none of the others would be nagging or writing angry letters or keeping you hung up on the phone while your TV dinner burned. On the other hand if you wanted to see any of them or talk to them that would be possible; you could go over to Ella's and see them any time because what that beam did was freeze them stiff, they were cool as cucumbers and stock still right where he caught them, they looked like it didn't hurt a bit and I must say it looked real natural. They looked how should I say it, calm.

Shan was more or less watching me while I looked at them all: would I scream or was I going to be all right? Well I just turned to him and I said, cool as a cucumber, "It's all right, Shan, they were never any friends of mine."

Then I helped him carry his case of Forever brooches and the box of balloons out of Ella's house and put them in my car.

He was real pleased with my house when we got there because it's right near the town reservoir, and he liked his room that used to be my sister Cynthia's because he said it afforded him a real good view of the town. Then we put the box of balloons and the case of brooches in the corner and he said, How can I ever thank you, and I blushed and pointed to the brooches and told him I would like one of them. It was in the shape of an elephant tusk, all studded with emeralds and diamonds, and I went all shivery when he pinned it to the folds on the front of my Billie Burke cocktail dress. Then he gave me a balloon for my very own living room and he was so grateful to me for helping him escape that he said he was going to tell me all about his mission, except he called it Our Mission, right after we ate, and I said, Shan, honey, that's just wonderful.

Well after supper it didn't turn out just the way he thought, and come to think of it, I'm just as glad. What he did was, he asked me for a list of my friends, you know, for the party? and I would rather die than admit to him that I didn't have any, I mean my whole mortal acquaintance was frozen cold and stiff back there at Ella Kemper's house and besides, I didn't really think that business about poisoning the water was such a good idea, I mean, it wasn't very *nice* and I would feel just terrible, but there was no way to tell him that, so while he was making plans and finishing his Royal icebox cheese-cake with the strawberry preserves, I got around where he couldn't see what I was doing, and I found the right stone to press and let him have it with the brooch.

It's real nice to have somebody here to eat my meals with and talk to when I feel like it, he looks real natural setting up there in the chair, and I have a pretty good idea that even though he's as stiff as one of them giant elephant tusks, he can still hear. He's got a real pleasant expression on him, kind of surprised, and the two of us have nice talks because he never ever disagrees. The other nice thing is he doesn't mess up the house any or dirty any laundry, and what's more he never complains about my cooking, the way Cynthia always did. If I ever figure out how to unfreeze him and I want to make toast for him, I just know he would eat it all the way a person is supposed to, instead of from the middle out, and what's more he would never, ever leave his crusts.

Chicken Soup

When he was little Harry loved being sick. He would stay in bed with his books and toys spread out on the blankets and wait for his mother to bring him things. She would come in with orange juice and aspirin at midmorning; at lunchtime she always brought him chicken soup with floating island for dessert, and when he had eaten she would straighten the pillow and smooth his covers and settle him for his nap. As long as he was sick he could stay in this nest of his own devising, safe from schoolmates' teasing and teachers who might lose their tempers, and falling down and getting hurt. He could wake up and read or drowse in front of the television, perfectly content. Some time late in the afternoon when his throat was scratchy and boredom was threatening his contentment, he would start watching the bedroom door. The shadows would be long by that time and Harry restless and perhaps faintly threatened by longer shadows that lurked outside his safe little room, the first intimations of anxiety, accident and risk. Finally he would hear her step on the stair, the clink of ice in their best glass pitcher, and she would come in with cookies and lemonade. He would gulp the first glass all at once and then, while she poured him another, he would feel his own forehead in hopes it would be hot enough to entitle him to another day. He would say: I think my head is hot. What do you think? She would touch his forehead in loving complicity. Then the two of them would sit there together, Harry and Mommy, happy as happy in the snug world they had made.

Harry's father had left his widow well fixed, which meant Mommy didn't have to have a job, so she had all the time in the world to make the house pretty and cook beautiful meals for Harry and do everything he needed even when he wasn't sick. She would wake him early so they could sit down to a good hot breakfast together, pancakes with sausage and orange juice, after which they would read to each other out of the paper until it was time for Harry to go. They always talked over the day when he came home from school and then, being a good mother, she would say, Don't you want to play with a little friend? She always made cookies when his friends came over, rolling out the dough and cutting it in neat circles with the rim of a wineglass dusted with sugar. She sat in the front row at every violin and flute recital, and when Harry had trouble with a teacher, any kind of trouble at all, she would go up to the grammar school and have it out with him. Harry's bed was made for him and his lunches carefully wrapped, and although nobody would find out until they reached middle school and took communal showers, Harry's mother ironed his underwear. In return Harry emptied the garbage and made the phone calls and did most of the things the man of the house would have done, if he had been there.

Like all happy couples they had their fights, which lasted only an hour or two and cleared the air nicely. Usually they ended with one of them apologizing and the other saying, with admirable largesse, I forgive you. In fact the only bad patch they had came in the spring the year Harry was twelve, when Charles appeared with a bottle of wine and an old college yearbook in which he and Harry's father were featured. Naturally Mommy invited him to dinner and Harry was shocked to come out of the kitchen with the bottle opener just in time to hear his mother saying, "You don't know what a relief it is to have an adult to talk to for a change."

Didn't Harry get asthma that night, and wasn't he home sick for the rest of the week? He did not spend his usual happy sick time because his mother seemed distracted almost to the point of being neglectful, and he was absolutely astonished at lemonade time that Friday. There were two sets of footsteps on the stairs.

Mommy came in first. "Oh Harry, I have a surprise for you."

"I'm too sick."

She managed to keep the smile in her voice. "It's Charles. He's brought you a present."

"I don't want it." He flopped on his stomach and put the pillows over his head.

"Oh Harry."

"Let me handle this." There was Charles's voice in his bedroom, his *bedroom,* that had always been sacrosanct. Harry wanted to rage and drive him out, he might even brain him with a bookend, but that would involve showing himself, and as long as he stayed under the pillows there was the chance Charles would give up and go away.

There was something wriggling on his bed.

"Help. What's that?"

"It's a puppy."

"Go away."

"Charles has brought you a lovely puppy."

"A puppy?"

There it was. He was so busy playing with it that he only half-heard when Mommy said the puppy's name was Ralph and Ralph was going to keep him company while she and Charles went out for a little while. Wait, Harry said, or tried to, but the puppy was warm under his hands and he couldn't keep his mind on what he was saying. It had already wet the blanket, and Harry was riveted by the experience. The wet was soaking right through the blanket and the sheet and into Harry's pajama leg, and by the time he had responded to the horror and the wonder of it, Mommy had already kissed him and she and Charles were gone.

For the first hour or two he and the puppy were happy together, but just as he began to take it into his confidence, convincing himself that it was company enough, the puppy flopped on its side and slept like a stone, leaving Harry alone in the room, jabbering to the gathering shadows. He clutched the covers under his chin and kept on talking, but the empty house was terrifying in its silence, so that Harry too fell silent, certain that both he and the house were listening.

She took forever to come home. When she did come in she was voluble and glowing, absently noting that she had forgotten to leave him anything for supper, passing it off with a halfhearted apology and a long recital of everything Charles had said and thought. She approached the bed with the air of a jeweler unveiling his finest creation and proffered a piece of Black Forest cake she had wrapped carefully right there in the restaurant and brought halfway across town cradled in her lap.

Harry did the only logical thing under the circumstances. He started wheezing. The puppy woke and blundered across the blanket to butt him with its head. He picked it up, murmuring to it between wheezes.

"Harry, Harry, what's the matter?"

He said, to the puppy, "I told you I was sick."

"Harry, please!" She proffered cough medicine and he spurned it; she held out the inhaler and he knocked it away.

He said, not to her, but to the puppy, "Mommy left me alone when I was sick."

"Harry, please."

"Right, puppy?"

"Oh Harry, please take your medicine."

"It's you and me, puppy. You and me."

Harry and the puppy were thick as thieves for the next couple of days. They refused to read the paper with his mother when she came in with breakfast and they wouldn't touch anything on any of her trays. Instead they bided their time and sneaked down to raid the kitchen when she was asleep. They talked only to each other, refusing all her advances, brooking no excuses and no apologies.

On the third day she cracked. She came to Harry's room empty-handed and weeping. "All right, what do you want me to do?"

He answered in a flash. "Never leave me alone when I'm sick."

"Is that all?"

"I don't like that guy."

"Charles?"

"I don't like him."

Her face was a study: whatever she felt for Charles in a tug-of-war with the ancient, visceral pull. After a pause she said, "I don't like him either."

Harry smiled. "Mommy, I'm hungry."

"I'll bring you a nice bowl of chicken soup."

That was the end of Charles.

After that Harry and his mother were closer than ever. If it cost her anything to say goodbye to romance she was gallant about it and kept her feelings well hidden. There was Harry to think about. She was the one who argued with his teachers over that last quarter of a point and prepped him for tests and sent the coach packing when he suggested that, with his build, Harry was a natural for basketball, and if Harry seemed at all reluctant to give up the team trips, boys and girls together on a dark and crowded bus, his mother pointed out that it would be the worst possible thing for his asthma. It was his mother who badgered the dean of admissions until Harry was enrolled in the college of his choice, located a convenient three blocks from their house. They were both astonished when, at the end of the first term, the dean suggested that he take a year off because he needed to mature. Harry and his mother talked about it privately and concluded that for whatever reasons, the administration objected to the presence of a middle-aged woman, however attractive, at the college hangout and in various seminars and waiting with Harry on the bench outside the dean's office until it was his turn to go in.

"Who needs college?" she said.

Harry thought, but did not say: Hey, wait.

"After all," she was saying. "We both know you're going to be an artist."

Harry was not so sure. His mother had enrolled him in the class because she had always wanted art lessons and so she assumed he would want them too, and Harry dutifully went to the Institute on Tuesdays to do still lifes of fruit of the season with the same old clay wine bottle in pencil, charcoal, pastels and acrylics. His colors all ran together and the shapes were hideous, but his mother admired them all the same.

"Oh Harry," she would say, promiscuous in her approval, "that's just beautiful."

"That's what you always say." It irritated him because it meant nothing, so that he was both flattered and fascinated when the cute girl from the next class came in just as he was finishing a depressing oil of that same old wine bottle, with dead leaves and acorns this time, and said, in hushed tones:

"Gee, that really stinks."

"Do you really think so?"

"Sorry, I just . . ."

"You're the first person who's ever told the truth. What's your name?"

"Marianne."

Harry fell in love with her.

It was around this time that his mother began to get on his nerves. If he lingered after class to talk to Marianne or buy her a cup of coffee, his mother would spring out the front door before he put his key in the lock. She would be a one-woman pageant of anxiety: Where have you been, What kept you, I thought you'd been hit by a taxi or run over by a truck, oh Harry, don't frighten me like that again. He would say, Aw, Ma, but she would already be saying: The least you could do is call when you're going to be late. She managed to be in the hall every time he used the phone, and when he began to go out with Marianne she could not keep herself from asking where he was going, how long he would be; it didn't matter whether he came home at 10 or 12 or 2 or 4 A.M., she would be rattling in the kitchen, her voice would take on the high hum of hysteria: I couldn't sleep.

He should have known better than to bring Marianne home to meet her. She didn't do much; she didn't say much, but she brought in his puppy, which was no longer a puppy but instead was aging, balding, with broken, rotting teeth. When Harry squatted to pet the dog his mother looked at Marianne over his head. "That's the only thing Harry has ever loved. Can't sleep without him."

Marianne looked at her in shock. "What?"

"Right next to him on the pillow, too. Head to head. I tried to get him to put that thing in the cellar, but all I have to do is mention it and Harry starts to wheeze."

"Harry wheezes?"

"Oh all the time," his mother said cheerfully, opening the front door for her.

When she was gone, Harry turned on his mother in a rage, but she managed to stop him in his tracks. "I only do these things because I love you. Think of what I have given up for you." She was wheezing herself, as she confronted him with their whole past history in her face.

"Oh Mother. I."

"I don't like Marianne."

All their years together accumulated and piled into him like the cars of a fast express. "I don't like her either," he said.

At the same time he knew he could not stand the force of his mother's love, wanted to leave her because he was suffocating, did not know how. He didn't know whether he would ever find another girl who loved him, but if he did, he was going to handle it differently.

His first vain thought was to marry his mother off, but she would not even accept a date. "You might need me," she said, in spite of all his protests that he was grown now, would do fine without her. "I wouldn't do that to you."

It was implied that he wouldn't do that to her, either, but he would in a flash, if he could only figure out how. It was around this time that he started going into the library in the evenings, and it was natural that he should find himself attracted to one of the librarians. She liked him too, and they had a nice thing going there in the stacks, late-night sandwiches and hurried kisses, but one night Harry heard a distinct rustling in the next aisle, and when he came around the end of Q–S and into T–Z he found his mother crouching, just as the girl he had been fondling saw her and began to scream . . .

When he stamped into the house that night she greeted him with a big smile and an apple pie.

"Mother, how could you?"

"Look, Harry, I baked this for you. Your favorite."

"How could you do a thing like that?"

"Why Harry, you know I would do anything for you."

"But you . . . damn . . . ruined . . ." He was frothing, raging and inarticulate. He looked into that face suffused by blind mother love and in his fury took desperate measures to dramatize his anger and frustration. "You . . ." He snatched the pie from her, ignoring her craven smile. "Have . . ." He raised it above his head, overriding her hurried it's-your-favorite, and screamed: "Got to stop." He took the fruit of her loving labor and dashed it to the floor.

There.

He was exhausted, quivering and triumphant. He had made her understand. She had to understand.

When the red film cleared and he could see again she was on her hands and knees in front of him, scraping bits of pie off the rug as if nothing would make her happier. "Oh Harry," she said, imperturbable in her love, "you know I would do anything for you."

A less determined son would have given up at that point, sinking into the morass of mother love, but two things happened to Harry at that time, each peculiarly liberating. First his puppy died. Then they began life classes at the Institute and Harry, who up to that point had seen only selected fragments of his mother, saw his first woman nude.

Her name was Coral and he fell in love with her. They began to stay after class, Harry pretending to keep sketching, Coral pretending to pose, until the night their hands met as he pretended to adjust her drape, and Coral murmured into his ear and Harry took her home. He may have been aware of rustling in the bushes outside the studio, or of somebody following as they went up the drive to Coral's bungalow, he may have sensed a determined, feral presence under Coral's bedroom window, but he tried to push back the awareness, to begin that which Coral appeared to be so ready to begin. He would have, too, kissing her as he took off his shirt, but as he clasped her to him Coral went rigid and began to scream. He turned quickly to see what had frightened her and although he caught only a glimpse of the face in the window it was enough.

"Harry, what is it?"

He lied. "Only a prowler. I think it's gone." He knew it wasn't.

"Then kiss me."

"I can't." He just couldn't.

"Please."

"I can't—yet. There's something I have to take care of."

"Don't go."

"I have to."

"When will you come back?"

"As soon as I can. It may not be until tomorrow."

"Tomorrow, then." Gradually, she let go. "Tomorrow or never, Harry. I don't wait."

"I promise." He was buttoning his shirt. "But right now there's something I have to do."

She was waiting for him at the end of the driveway, proffering something. He didn't know how she had gotten there because he had taken the car; he had the idea she might have run the whole way because she was breathing hard and her clothes were matted with brambles; her stockings were torn and muddy at the knees. Her face was a confusing mixture of love and apprehension, and as he came toward her she shrank.

"I thought you might need your sweater."

He looked at her without speaking.

"I only do these things because I love you."

He opened the car door.

"Harry, you know I'd do anything for you."

He still did not speak.

"If you're mad at me, go ahead and get good and mad at me. You know I'll forgive you, no matter what you do."

"Get in."

She made one more stab. "It's raining, Harry. I thought you might be cold."

Later, when they made the turn away from their house and up the road into the foothills, she said, "Harry, where are we going? Where are you taking me?"

His response was dredged from millennia of parent-child dialogues. He leaned forward, taking the car into rocky, forbidding country, up an increasingly sharp grade. He said, "We'll see."

Maybe he only planned to frighten her, but at that last, terrible moment she said, blindly, "I'll always be there when you need me."

He got rid of her by pushing her into Dumbman's Gorge. She got right out of the car when he told her to, she would have done anything to keep on his right side, and when he pushed her she looked back over her shoulder with an inexorable motherly smile. There were dozens of jagged tree stumps and sharp projecting rocks and she seemed to ricochet off every single one of them going down but in spite of that, and perhaps because of the purity of the air and the enormous distance she had to tumble, he thought he heard her calling to him over her shoulder: I forgive you, the words trailing behind her in a dying fall.

He didn't know whether it was guilt or the simple result of going all the way to the peak above Dumbman's Gorge and standing out there arguing in such rotten weather, but he was sick by the next evening, either flu or pneumonia, and there was no going to Coral's house that evening to take his reward. He telephoned her instead and she came to him, looking hurried and distracted and shying off when he began to cough and sneeze.

"I really want to, Harry, but right now you're too contagious."

"But Coral." He could hardly breathe.

"As soon as you get better." She closed the bedroom door behind her.

When he tried to get up to plead with her he found he was too weak to stand. "But Coral," he said feebly from his bed.

"I'll lock the front door behind me," she said, her voice rising behind her as she descended the stairs. "Do you want some chicken soup?"

His voice was thin but he managed to say, "Anything but that."

He heard the thump as she closed the front door.

Despairing, he fell into a fevered sleep.

It may have been partly the depression of illness, the frustration of having his triumph with Coral postponed, it may have been partly delirium and partly the newly perceived flickering just beyond the circle of his vision: the gathering shadows of mortality. It may only have been a sound that woke him. All Harry knew was that he woke suddenly around midnight, gasping for breath and sitting bolt upright, swaying in the dark. He was paralyzed, trembling in the fearful certainty that something ominous was approaching, coming slowly from a long way off. When he found that his trunk could not support itself and his legs would no longer move he sank back into the pillows, bloating with dread.

There had been a sound: something on the walk, sliding heavily and falling against the front door.

I came as soon as I could.

"What?" Why couldn't he sit up?

He did not know how much time passed but whatever it was, it was in the house now. It seemed to be dragging itself through the downstairs hall. Was that it in the kitchen? In his terror and delirium he may have blacked out. He came to, returning from nowhere, thought he might have been hallucinating, tried to slow his heart. Then he heard it again. It was on the stairs leading to his room, mounting tortuously.

You're sick.

"My God." He tried to move.

The sound was in the hall outside his room now, parts of whatever it was were thumping or sliding wetly against his bedroom door in a travesty of a knock. In another second it would start to fumble with the knob. He cried out in terrible foreknowledge: "Who's there?"

Harry, it's Mother.

Final Tribute

Now Jane and I went down to Washington on the bus and we took our kids so they could tell their grandchildren, even though they were too little to remember. Donny's funeral was bigger than Elvis Presley's even, or any of those presidents or popes or kings, he was after all the first rock star to become President, and I was at that funeral. We had to ride all day and night to get there and I almost lost my best friend, but I was there. I had on my Cheryl Tiegs jeans with the matching shirt and my great-grandmother's gold bracelet that she fished out of the ashes after the Chicago fire, that bracelet tied me to a thread of history that started way back, and will continue. My mother saw President Roosevelt when she was little, her Daddy held her up when his car went past the park where they were waiting. She isn't sure which one he was but she will never forget it; she knows she is forever part of history.

In addition to which, there was the grief. We felt so terrible about Donny dying that we had to do something.

I will never forget what I was doing when we got the news. Everything was so ordinary, Bud and me getting up and having scrambled eggs, me putting cupcakes in his lunch. I had little Buddy in his sunsuit and my girlfriend Jane came over so we could pin hems in these skirts we were making. Both babies were in the playpen and the sun was coming in, Jane was up on a chair and nobody had a thought except how hot it was, and where the next pin was going. Jane had on her lavender T-shirt like my aqua one, I had great-grandmother's bracelet pushed up on my arm to keep it from clanking and there was the TV saying he had died.

At first we didn't believe it. He was so young and he didn't get shot like John Lennon or the Kennedys and he didn't OD like Janis and Jimi and them, he just got sick and died, it was amazing.

We couldn't say anything. I just started taking the pins out of my mouth and laying them down so all the ends were pointing the same way, and when I had them just right I said to Jane:

Did you hear that?

I don't think so.

Me either.

Then Jane put her hand on my shoulder and her voice was shaking. I think I better get down off this chair.

The TV went on like it had never happened, the band was playing because this lady had taken the curtain and won a car and a trip to Florida, and for a minute we could pretend we hadn't heard it. Then they came back with a statement from the doctors and pictures of him as a baby, so we knew there was no pretending. We could not stop crying. It seemed like the whole world was crying, the TV showed people crying in eleven different cities, it made you want to run out in the streets and be with them. A terrible thing like that makes you want to do something. Even if you are only two small-town married girls with babies, you want to do something.

So it was providence when Clarada telephoned. She is still working downtown so we don't see her much, she can afford a neat car and pretty clothes that we can't, so it was nice of her to remember us. She wanted us to know they were going to have the body lying in state in Washington and our town was chartering a bus. I couldn't get hold of Bud at work and Jane and Ed are separated anyway, so we packed some food and the diaper bags and I left Bud a note. We took raincoats and our cassette players with the phones along with all of Donny's hits so we would be prepared for anything. Then we went down to City Hall with our deposit bottle money and bought places on the bus.

We were lucky because Mr. Edgar was in charge, that used to be our high school civics teacher. Way back in the beginning he used to play Donny's records in class and once he took our class all the way to Albany for the first demonstration. He had a clipboard and a Donny button from, I don't know if it was the last concert or the last campaign, and he sold us the last two seats on the bus so I guess he recognized us. There was only one bathroom in the back and we were going to have to ride all day and all night to get there, but we would be first in line at the cathedral next morning, along with a hundred thousand others.

Jane climbed in next to the window with baby Eddy and all our stuff and this terribly nice guy from across the aisle fell all over himself helping her. Then I had to ask him to move so baby Buddy and I could sit down. We came out in such a rush that we were not necessarily looking our best when Clarada came and spoke to us. She had on a dark cotton with shoes in complementary colors and I could see what she was thinking. Here we were moving the earth to get to this funeral, my mother saw President Roosevelt when she was little and I was wearing my great-grandmother's gold bracelet, me, that had hitchhiked five hundred miles to hear Donny in concert, so who was she to worry about appearances.

I said, It's hard to get moving when you have babies to think of.

She said, So glad you could make it, but that was not what she meant.

It's what's in our hearts that counts.

Oh well, maybe nobody will notice.

You don't have any right to say who is worthy.

She smiled this poison smile: When Donny was in Syracuse I ran up on the stage and handed him a flower.

I could feel Jane shivering next to me. Then she said this astonishing thing: He stopped at my father's gas station once?

Jane!

Who did?

Donny. His car broke down on his way back from Syracuse.

Oh Jane. There she was, pretty Jane Snyder, my best friend, throwing back her long blonde hair and telling the world, me and Clarada and this cute guy from across the aisle.

I bet, Clarada said. He kissed the flower I threw to him and gave it back to me, I keep it in this locket. Then she showed us this brown-looking thing she wore around her neck, it could have been anything.

Jane's voice was so soft you could pretend you hadn't heard: He talked to me while my father fixed his motor.

I don't know why this made me feel betrayed.

Whatever Clarada was about to say got lost because the bus lurched and Mr. Edgar said everybody had to sit down so we could get going. I could feel my heart climbing up and I hugged baby

Buddy. Even though I was too excited to breathe I couldn't stop thinking about Jane, and what she said, so I leaned over to her and whispered: Is it true what you told them about Donny?

Jane just smiled and didn't answer.

About ten minutes Clarada was bumping our way, heading back to the bathroom. She managed to lurch into the guy across the aisle, so he would hear what she told us: After Donny kissed the rose he invited me backstage.

Yeah, show us your plaster cast.

Clarada just ignored me.

When his car broke down it took two days to get it fixed, Jane said in this dreamy voice. Two whole days. Then she got out her paper bag and said, Maybe it's time for the sandwiches. She found a really messy one with lots of salami and lettuce hanging down and said, What about it, Clarada, want one of our sandwiches?

You'd think it was a snake.

She might get mustard on her fancy dress, I said, and started laughing, but I will admit there was this uneasy feeling stirring. You can tell me the truth, I said to Jane under my breath. Is that the truth about Donny?

That's for me to know and her to find out.

You never told me.

Never mind, Jane said, and put baby Eddy between us.

I am a happily married woman but sitting there like that I felt like I'd been left standing in the road. First I lost Donny, that I had counted on to sing me through and defend our country for me, and now there was this with Jane, that I have been best friends with since the sixth grade. I kept turning the bracelet on my wrist and getting broody: twenty-eight years old and I have never done a single wild thing. At least I had the bracelet. There is something about gold. It may not turn a person on but it can keep the motor running. I remember figuring, well, this thing came out of the Chicago fire, my mother saw President Roosevelt in real life and by God I am going to this funeral.

After a while Jane moved Eddy to her other shoulder. I couldn't be sure whether she was looking my way or trying to catch somebody else's eye, you know, across the aisle, but I took the chance to speak to her.

Jane, what do you think about everything?

I think it's terribly sad.

No. I got her eye and would not let go. I mean the rest. That story you were telling.

I think you're upset and I'm upset.

But we're best friends, aren't we?

We've always been best friends, Jane said, we wear each other's clothes. I have on your purple jeans right now, she said, but she didn't have her mind on it.

You never told me about Donny and the gas station.

Oh that, she said. There wasn't any point to it.

You won't even say if it's true.

What does it matter? We're best friends anyway.

Even with the babies stuck between us, I knew she was smiling. I moved little Buddy around on my front so I could put my face in his hair and try to pretend it didn't matter. When it started to get dark outside Mr. Edgar handed out the armbands and the maps, with dotted lines from the parking lot to the cathedral. Then somebody started singing and pretty soon we were all singing Donny's favorites, at least all the ones we could sing without crying. Some of them are just too private and important. The first time Jane and I heard Donny sing we were in the sixth grade and I will never forget the way my insides jumped up, it was like discovering sex, but more lasting. Around ten o'clock Mr. Edgar got up in the front and made a little speech, about how to form up and what to do when we got to the cathedral. Then he told us to remember who we were, he wanted us to be fresh in the morning so we would be a credit to our city. The reverend led us in prayer after which they dimmed the lights because we were supposed to go to sleep.

Some did, I suppose, but Jane and I were too excited. The kids were like little rocks planted on our fronts and we rode along in the dark with our eyes wide open. After a while Jane started talking in a low voice; I kept my voice down too because those were not exactly prayers we were reciting but the whole thing—the bus, all of us riding down there in the dark, with one or two murmuring—it was kind of like church. You had to be there to understand it.

I was always in love with him.

Oh Jane, me too.

He stood between me and Ed. He was always in the bed with us.

I know what you mean. I didn't explain to her, but Bud has this hair growing out of a mole that really bothers me and when we make love his eyes will not stop running.

She said: but you are happily married.

Married is not enough.

Nothing is.

At least we are going to the funeral.

Poor Jane, she said: I would like to get in the grave with him. I mean, after everything.

If she was not going to tell me what happened with her and Donny or if it even happened, I certainly was not going to ask. Instead I said: Hey Jane, you know this gold bracelet I am wearing?

I know, the Chicago fire.

Plus which my mother saw President Roosevelt in person. And now we are going to the funeral.

Next to Donny President Roosevelt is nothing.

Please don't bring that up again.

I just feel so terrible.

Shut up and go to sleep, I said, and then I pretended to. Maybe I did. It was the middle of the night before I knew it. Then I put Buddy down and went to the bathroom in the back. The funny thing was, when I was done I couldn't find my seat. I kept going back and forth in the dark until finally I figured it out. My seat was right there, tenth from the back on the right, but there was somebody in it.

You're in my seat.

It was the guy from across the aisle. He pretended to be asleep but when I poked him he whispered, You can have mine, it's empty.

What have you done with Buddy?

Jane said, He's laying over there. Stephen moved him.

You left him alone. You left baby Buddy alone. I blundered in the dark and almost sat on him, they had just laid him over there without a care for how he landed. Oh Jane, how could you?

Hush.

That's no way to treat a baby.

It's all right, she said, the bitch. He isn't a baby.

By that time everybody was shishing me. I picked up the baby and held him tight in Stephen's seat and I could not stop crying.

In the morning Clarada came clacking down the aisle on the way to the bathroom to finish her makeup. I don't know where or how she got changed but she had on this dark purple cotton with covered purple buttons all the way up to the neck and a black belt that went with her armband, you would think she was the widow. When she saw the way things were I guess she couldn't stand it. There was Jane with this cute guy Stephen and baby Eddy stuffed in next to the window so Stephen could keep his arm around her, they were cuddling.

Clarada said, That's obscene. Donny isn't even in the ground.

Jane didn't say anything.

So Clarada leaned over the two of them and started yelling. Donny and I were together in Syracuse, we were in bed for three days and three nights and we did not stop loving.

Jane just snuggled in the crook of this Stephen's arm and wouldn't speak to her.

Clarada kept on yelling. You said you were with Donny. I say it's a lie.

Oh that, Jane said. You can have that. I don't need it.

I wanted to push Clarada out of the way and pull on Jane's hand until she answered. Was it? Was it a lie? By that time I knew she was never going to answer. What's more she wasn't even going to line up with me at the funeral. By the time the bus stopped and we all got off, I had completely lost sight of her. One minute Clarada was getting ready to punch Jane and Mr. Edgar was calling for order, and the next we were surging off the bus.

It was like being at the end of the world, or the beginning. There were at least five bands that I counted just on the street where the bus dumped us, plus a horse guard and a bunch of Moonies and some Hare Krishnas and a whole gang of Marines, maybe they were there to keep order but half of them were wearing Donny wigs and the other half were crying. There were a lot of Donny lookalikes and heads of Donny fan clubs and politicos and I heard that the line of limousines started back down in front of the White House, heads of state that had come from all over the world for the funeral. We were going to have a couple of days of him lying in state and the presidents and kings would go inside and the rest of us could listen to it over the loudspeakers. I have never heard so much wailing or seen so

many banners. It was about the nicest place I've ever been because
nobody was ugly or unruly, we were all in it together and we all just
kind of shuffled forward until we got to the cathedral walk where the
Marines formed everybody up twelve across so they could go down
the walk and into the big double doors where people were lined up
waiting to file past Donny's casket.

It took me all day. By the time I got up front I had lost sight of
every single soul I knew and I had almost run out of bagels to keep
baby Buddy quiet. I thought I was never going to get there and the
next minute I was inside. It was the strangest thing. Out there on the
walk with a hundred thousand people milling, I felt betrayed and
bereft. My best friend that I thought I knew was off with this strange
guy doing God knows what and I had lost Donny forever. The next
minute I was inside and I felt wonderful.

Maybe it was being inside the church, there were banners along
the side aisles and light coming in colored strips through the stained
glass windows, everybody was going along with their heads bowed in
peace and quiet, but there was a lot more to it than that. What
happened was, the Marines peeled us off in rows of two so we could
file down the aisle in two lines going on either side of the casket. I
had a chance to look around at the other people, all the other different kinds of faces and the many things they had chosen to wear,
everything from all black to street clothes to shiny disco costumes,
and that was wonderful, and so many of us that were so different all
being there in the same place doing the same thing was wonderful. I
waited forever and then I was there and I looked down at Donny in
the casket, that sweet dead face, and my heart jumped up. I thought:
That is you lying there dead instead of me, which is what heroes are
for, and the thought made me so joyful that I had to do something to
thank him.

I did it so fast that nobody saw. I just shook my arm and it slid
right off my hand into the space between his shoulder in the white
tuxedo and the blue satin side of the casket.

There you go, I said. You and Jane either did or didn't, it doesn't
matter a damn because you are going to be buried with my great-
grandmother's bracelet.

I never did find out the truth about him and Jane, I never even found out what happened with that cute guy Stephen, because by the time the funeral was over he was gone and she rode back in the seat next to me. To tell the truth, it doesn't matter.

Into the Parlor

If she could just get it right she would begin to hear their voices: handsome Jim and Philip, Ada and Cecelia on that brilliant afternoon, the twins; all her brothers and sisters planted like so many flowers at Mama's feet while May herself drifted—no; once she got it back she would make it right.

On Sundays they used to bend their heads over the midday dinner, all the starches, the three kinds of pie; then Papa would rise, groaning, and lead the way into the parlor, where the afternoon sun lay in golden stripes across the carpet and flecks of dust hung in the light. Little Ada always went to the piano and played while the others sang and May herself lay on her stomach on the love seat, listening. She held her breath and pressed her face to the upholstery in a passion, as if she could absorb all of it: the flamestitch pattern in shades of gold, the sunlight, their life in the big old house on Winter Street where nobody was ever lonely, or sad.

If she closed her eyes now she could bring back the pattern, and along with it all the objects in the parlor: the Florentine china clock and Mama's rose-encrusted urns with the gold fluting and the gold-leafed bases and the Aubusson carpet and the damask draperies with the heavy gold fringe. If she lifted her face from the flamestitching today May imagined she would be able to see them all—dear Mama surrounded by the children, her jewels; Papa nodding in the doorway, keeping time, on that perfect Sunday when they were never happier. What had happened to all of it? She still thought she could bring it back and would, no matter what it cost her.

She could see it now, the room, and everything in it—the triangular vitrine on its gilded legs, the della Robbia plaque, the statue of Apollo that she loved so much; the pedestal was alabaster, she thought, and Ada had it, but Phil had taken the statue off to Arizona when the girls broke up the house, even though he knew May wanted it; it might not be Cellini, but it was certainly bronze. What else was there, that she had forgotten? Her sisters discarded the family treasures as carelessly as they spent their lives, heedless of what they had been given. Beautiful Ada ruined her figure and her singing voice with alcohol; Cecelia cheapened herself by working in a defense plant during the war and meeting the wrong kind of men, and to look at the twins now, nobody would guess that they had been debutantes, presented to society at the last Rose Petal Ball before the Crash. They had let all that go—who they were and what they had, and only May was left to take care of things.

Poor May, she did the best she could; she drove a thousand miles the year they sold the house to save what she could manage to take out of it. She was too late to prevent the auction but she sat down on Mama's love seat right in the middle of everything and would not let the movers carry it out. "Look at what you have," she cried to her sisters, "why can't you take care of what you have?"

"Life goes on," Cecelia said, ticking off items as the movers came and went.

"Remember the Christmas parties in the parlor, and dear old Beaufort in the kitchen, remember all the pies."

"Nobody can afford to keep this place," Cecelia said.

"Remember how we used to play in the cupola."

"It's a white elephant."

May was trembling at the outrage. "This was our home."

"Well it isn't any more," Cecelia said, and picked up one of Mama's rose-encrusted urns and carried it out. Ada took the other before May could even gather breath to speak.

"May you'd better get up off the love seat so the gentlemen can move it." Ada was tapping her foot.

"No, I love it, and you knew I wanted it."

"That old thing? Who would want that? Oh hell, if it means that much to you take it." Ada motioned to the movers to set it aside.

"Phil always used to slide down the banister frontward," May said. "He would land on both feet at the bottom and pull my curls." She got up absently and wandered upstairs, opening doors as if she half-expected to come upon her brothers and sisters in childhood, playing in one of the empty rooms. She would join them and stay there forever. She wandered with her head cocked as if listening and she went into cupboards and under the stairs with a growing sense of purpose, in search of some central possession that she could not yet identify but that she knew was already missing, it had not gone off with the movers and was not standing out on the curb waiting for the rubbish truck, it was essential to what she was trying to do but she could not for the life of her figure out what it was.

She came into the empty parlor in the late afternoon and knew at once. The angle of light on the bare floor made a path to the spot where the statue of Apollo had stood for as long as she could remember; she used to lie just *so* on the love seat and watch the play of sunlight on the bronze thighs.

"All right," she said, confronting her sisters. "What happened to the Apollo?"

"Why, we gave it to Phil."

"You know Mama promised it to me."

"Mama no such thing."

"Well Phil has it," Ada said absently. At her back the movers were leaving with the vitrine.

"Oh stop it," May hurled herself at the piece of furniture, bringing it to earth. "I'll pay you for it, I'll give anything you want."

She would never understand why Ada was so angry. "If you don't stop that I'm going to kill you."

"I used to play dollhouse on the bottom shelf, and Jimmy would bring me candy and sometimes Mama came and played." Did she really sit down on the floor and begin to wail? "You were always Mama's favorite but I'm the only one who really cares."

Mama would be pleased, she knew. She saved the love seat and the chaise and several other pieces and moved heaven and earth to get them home. She got a carpet that looked almost enough like the Aubusson and had a carpenter make a wooden shelf that she painted white and had put up at the same height as the mantelpiece they had at home. It was just as well that her poor late husband Arthur was gone by that time because the place was crowded and there would not have been room for Mama's things along with Arthur's things. The big old furniture sat uneasily in her little bungalow, the bookcase that had been so magnificent in the hallway on Winter Street towered here, hulking over her tiny living room like a captive animal; the vitrine was crowded in a corner and in the bedroom her father's gun cabinet sulked.

Still when she wedged herself on the love seat and pressed her face into the flamestitching she could almost be in the wonderful time; if she squinted her eyes she could see the vitrine and in its glass front she could see reflected her family, her handsome brothers and sisters, the laden dinner table still visible through the dining-room arch; she could run out through the double doors into the garden where she might discover all of them, playing in the grass. When she was a girl they had spent leisurely Sundays on Daddy's yawl on the river, the girls had gone to luncheons during the summer and debutante teas on Saturday afternoons. They spent part of every August at the family summer cottage on Sea Island, and they were treated with respect no matter where they went because they were Daniel Allen's children, but when she went out now people often used language Mama never even imagined and she herself had not heard spoken aloud, and when she was called into the bank because of some checks that had been returned they did not treat her with respect.

She did not like to go out much any more. In her pretty living room, surrounded by all the Allen treasures, she could imagine life outside was more or less as it had been, because in those days the house was filled with family and friends, in every respect there was bounty, and nothing that had happened to any of them since could measure up. Her poor marriage: how could she explain to Arthur why moving away from home made her so lonely she wanted to cry? How could she replicate the Allen Sunday dinners when there were only the two of them to cook for, and frankly, Arthur did not provide as well as Papa had? How could she get him to share her wonderful memories, and how could she fill her and Arthur's house with people when they couldn't even have a baby, no matter how they tried? When she started talking about those Sundays at home he always looked cross and tired and when she would begin to tell him about Phil and the banister or Jimmy and the dollhouse in the vitrine he would simply go to sleep. At the end she was glad there were never any babies because Arthur did not leave her very well fixed. When her brother Jim was lost in the war it was a tragedy; Arthur's passing was quiet as a sigh.

Outside a superhighway knifed through the dry creek bed at the end of the block and cars came and went on an incessant loop; the neighborhood was going downhill and parts of it were no longer safe, but in her living room May could press her face to the flamestitching on the love seat and recover entire months out of her childhood, and when she got up she would take lemon oil and a soft cloth to all the rosewood and mahogany of her childhood and make it gleam. Her sisters had not taken care of their things. Poor Ada had been divorced for years and her children never came to visit because she was intoxicated half the time, she had put Mama's Minton china in the dishwasher so many times that all the gold was eaten away. Cecelia was ill and had a housekeeper who abused her, and when May went to visit she found Mama's beautiful silver tea service all brown with tarnish and buried in the cupboard behind some cleaning things. Jim was gone and the twins had both passed away, which was how May had come into the flamestitched fire-shield that matched the love seat, and the della Robbia plaque. One of her nephews had taken it to a junk dealer who told May, when she went to buy it back, that it was only a copy anyway.

It didn't matter. With the plaque in place she felt very close, and when—out of a clear sky—one of Ada's daughters sent her the rose-encrusted urns, which Ada had neglected terribly, she took it as a sign. Once they were in place only the statue of Apollo was missing; when she had restored it to the room she could forget about the ugly trouble with the bank and the attempted break-in; by the time they came to get her, she would be gone. Phil had the statue in Arizona; he never wrote and the one time Cecelia went to him for help with her hospital bills, he was mean.

May herself was not in particularly good health now; at least once a day her heart flopped over in her chest, and it was with a sense of painful haste that she took the last of her savings and flew out to Phil's.

Poor Phil was in ill health too; he seemed touched that she had come all this way.

"Oh Phil, we used to have such wonderful times." She had put on her best blue dress and put a blue rinse in her hair and looked almost pretty, she thought. It was like going to a party, being here. "You were the handsomest boy . . ."

"Things happen," her brother said and put on his oxygen mask.

"I remember how you used to slide down the banister feet first, and go thump at the bottom and pull my curls."

"I don't think so. I think that was Jim."

"And those wonderful dinners Beaufort made for us, with the roasts and all those creamed vegetables, and the sweet potato pie."

"Mother used to punish us for not eating enough. She made you fat and she made Ada fat."

"And the cakes," May said. "Beaufort always saved me an extra piece of cake."

"I always hated Beaufort," Phil said.

So she had to stop going around the long way and confront him. "I came for the statue, Mama said it was mine."

"She said no such thing." Phil was gasping behind the mask.

When they were little he used to grab her wrists and pinch until she let go of the candy, or whatever it was, but she was stronger now. "You're too sick to take proper care of it."

She was exhausted by the time she got the statue home and had it unpacked. If she could only get it right she would begin to hear their voices, but even before she lay down on the love seat she knew something was wrong. She had to be able to turn her head just *so* and see the afternoon sunlight gilding the muscles of the thighs. She knew it was at the wrong height and she was going to have to have the pedestal; the last time she saw it, Ada had a Boston fern sitting on top and there were water stains in the alabaster, spreading all the way down to the base.

When she came into her sister's house after the long drive she realized she was shaken by the trip and blinking, already put off by the clutter and the smell. Ada's bony hands fluttered across her face and it made May weep to see how badly she had failed. "If you'd told me you were coming I would have fixed myself up."

"Oh Ada, you look fine." May hugged her close to hide the lie.

"I suppose you came for the pedestal."

"You've heard from Phil?"

"He was beside himself. But then he always was cross as a bear."

"Remember how we used to tease him about his girlfriends?" May tipped her head back with a little laugh. "And how his friends used to come over, just to talk to you . . ."

Ada sighed. "That was a long time ago."

"Not necessarily." May looked around at the poverty of the room: the shabby sofa, the stains in the carpet, one of their mother's glass paperweights covering a crack in the window and in the corner the pedestal, the last pretty thing her sister had. "Oh Ada, we should have taken better care of things."

"It's going to have to be wrapped."

"Oh Ada, we never should have let it slip away."

"I have a man coming to fix it so you can take it in the car."

"Ada, you shouldn't." May put both hands to her face. "I think you should keep it for yourself. You need a few pretty things."

Ada's hand faltered but her voice was firm. "My eyes aren't good enough to see it anyway."

"I'll never forget you for this." Her voice was strangely light. "And don't worry. I'll get it back for you." She was not certain of her intentions or how she was going to carry them out but the promise embraced all of them—the Allens—and everything they'd had.

Once she got it right she did indeed begin to hear their voices: even Jim, who had been killed in the war. She heard Jim and Philip, Ada and Cecelia and the twins; the voices were faint but present as soon as she unpacked the pedestal and put the statue in its place. Once she lay down on the sofa she would get it back. Excited as she was, she waited long enough to stop the mail delivery and have the utilities shut off. Then she turned Arthur's picture to the light and made her farewells without regret. She would not even remember him where she was going; it would be as if her life since then had never been. In the living room, she ran her hands over the Apollo and then folded herself on the love seat and closed her eyes, wondering how long she would have to wait.

In the next second, she was back. Little Ada was playing, slightly off key, while her brothers punched and wrestled in the background and Mama frowned. The twins lay under the piano, stuffed and logy from too many kinds of pie and May herself felt slightly queasy, felt it so strongly that she began to wonder whether she was going to have to let go here, or try to make it out of the room.

There was a sudden weight on her back and she writhed, fighting free of Phil, who had let go of Jim and was tormenting her. She got to her feet then, grappling with him in spite of the nausea and the constricted feeling left by recent tears. They swayed and fell on the rug and before May could recover herself or remember why she had been crying she was aware of Mama standing over her, and heard the steel in Mama's voice.

"You," she said, not using May's name at all. "That's just one thing too many. Go to your room."

Then she looked up with everything in her eyes and in her heart and in her voice, crying, "It's me, Mama, here I am. I took good care of everything."

"Get up," Mama said, "and stop that foolishness."

"Oh Mama . . ."

"Now apologize to your brother."

She was slipping; she whined, "But it was his fault."

"Disobedient girl," Mama said, with an expression of such cold dislike that May shrank from it. "Aren't you ashamed?"

So she was going to throw up after all, and she hurled herself on the love seat and then turned, heaving, and spilled her misery on the rug.

When she recovered she looked up to find the room was empty, and much smaller, and for the moment this was a relief. Here she was in her own little living room; the rose-encrusted urns were on the wooden shelf instead of the old marble mantelpiece. She was May in old age and once she had cleaned up the mess on the rug with Glory everything would be all right. She sat up and considered.

It was the draperies, she decided after considerable thought. She never should have tried it without having the draperies in place. She could have some made and once she did, all she would need to do would be find or replicate the gold-leafed rosettes that held them back.

The Holdouts

Seen from a distance, it would have looked like something out of the funny papers: a small, overgrown island somewhere in the Pacific; wild trees encircling a place which was more nest than clearing, with a Japanese private standing guard over a dugout thatched in palm; he would be holding a rifle so rusty as to have no remaining moving parts, ready to defend his commanding officer and the adjutant who sat inside in tattered uniforms, incessantly moving markers across a packing crate in a game of GO. There would be signs of an enduring domesticity: vestigial uniforms freshly washed and hanging on a vine, marks in the bamboo uprights—hundreds of small nicks, the GO scores up to the point when the players tired of recording them; more than two dozen large nicks, marking off too many years. Their conversation would be almost visible: weary Japanese characters in ragged talk balloons, and over the private's head a vision of acres of complaisant bellies and embracing thighs. Of course they could not see themselves from a distance; they had lived so close for so many years that they could hardly see each other, and, offered the opportunity to see themselves from a distance, they would have refused because that would make it too hard for them to carry on, and this had been their duty: to fight when engaged and remain at this post until relieved; so far neither had happened and so they continued to carry on.

The worst part of all was the waiting.

In the beginning there had been plenty to do: enemy on all sides, blood filling the air in a misty spray, warlike din, cries of the wounded and shouts of Banzai, but when it was over and the captain and the lieutenant emerged to view the incredible carnage, there was an uncanny silence in the jungle; it was as if all other human life had ceased that day, and when they dragged themselves back to headquarters they found that, with a private named Kimu, whom they dragged out of the ruined hut, they were the only members of the Imperial Army left alive.

There was sure to be a second wave and so they had salvaged what they could and retreated to the jungle to prepare. When the enemy came they would be hopelessly outnumbered but they would take as many of the enemy with them as they could, dying gloriously and so winning after all, because this glorious death would fulfill all their lifetime aspirations.

Perhaps they would not die, but would emerge victorious to greet the landing forces. The marks of their suffering would be an inspiration to all.

Or the emperor, marking the glorious victory which would come in time would make a tour of these islands. He would commend them for their fidelity, admiring the military neatness of the encampment and the scale of discipline they had managed to maintain.

If they had to, they would die snuffing a Marine straggler or a single guerrilla, so achieving a soldier's most honorable aim.

In the meantime, they were beginning to get on each other's nerves. In the first months, or years, the main business had been survival, because they had received no more supplies. Yoshi, the lieutenant, would direct Private Kimu on foraging expeditions while Captain Shigamitsu worked over reports and thought up face-saving duties for himself because he was so excellent at delegating authority that he had left himself with nothing to do. Yoshi was ambitious and although he could not expect advancement so long as there were only three of them, he looked at Shigamitsu in obvious speculation, wondering just how long it would be before a venomous insect or a jungle disease carried their captain away. Kimu was lonely, and entertained fantasies in which he and the others would become comrades instead of commanders-and-subordinate. When it seemed safe enough they could build a fire and sit around a roasting pig, exchanging reminiscences of student days in the mother country, the snows on Mount Fuji, chimes tinkling like crystal in isolated shrines. He would tell them about Benji, the bride he had known for only two weeks before the war swept him up and carried him away, and they in turn would tell about their wives or women; they could build story on story and so make all the absences tolerable. But Yoshi would rebuff him and Shigamitsu was forever the commander, preoccupied and remote. When he was off duty Kimu could not hope to fraternize, and so he would take his loneliness to some safe spot where he could lie on his back and look through the branches at his hopes, so absorbed that he barely noticed the changing aircraft which moved faster and faster, lacing the sky. Back in camp, the lieutenant continually tried to better himself; Captain Shigamitsu secretly thought that Yoshi talked too much.

As the years passed they grew more and more adept at hunting iguanas and harvesting the fruit which presented itself in unlikely guises in the greenery. Captain Shigamitsu had, early on, relieved the private the duty of preparing the food. Now, in the interest of art, he spent hours over each meal, while Lieutenant Yoshi stitched new shoes for them out of vines and bark, and Private Kimu alternately stood guard and policed the area, burying rubbish and scraps because the captain still firmly believed that it was only a matter of time before the enemy arrived and they had to withdraw to a better vantage point without leaving a trace. They would ambush the enemy and fall on them like ravening beasts, killing in an orgy of fulfillment which would redeem all these years. Secretly, each admitted to himself that it was not such a bad existence. They had lived so long with waiting that now waiting was their life.

Every night of their lives Minnie had to go into the projection booth and run the unfinished *White Goddess* for the aging Alta McKay. Gorgeous in crushed velvet, the star would coil on her brocaded sofa, crying out each time she saw the plane crash in the jungle, weeping with relief when, as the golden-haired aviatrix, she emerged from the plane to rule over all those wonder-struck savages. Still she never could be happy because, just as the jealous witch-doctor approached her with his knife, the picture would flicker and give way to blank leader and she would bite her knuckles in frustration because this would have been her greatest picture, a monument to her love for LaMont Raburn, who, as Captain Gallant, had wooed her onscreen and off.

If she didn't get some money soon she was never going to finish *White Goddess.* Of course she would have to replace LaMont; he was in real estate in Encino now, he had a string of franchise chicken houses and although she seldom saw him she knew he had a paunch, the smooth skin and patient air of a man who has grown too old too soon. It was not, after all, LaMont but the *idea* of LaMont she had to be faithful to, and at the back of her mind flickered a picture of his replacement: tall and handsome and young. She herself would avoid closeups, doing her takes through gauze or a protective screen of leaves. She would invite LaMont to the premiere and rekindle the fires of their love, taking up life at the point at which it had been so cruelly broken off. It was like having a child half born; once it was done she could relax, she might even marry LaMont; they could grow fat off his fried chicken and she could let her face and her waistline go, she would at last be able to let herself grow old. But her prospects were poor and it was bitter, bitter to see the story broken off at this same point every night and not know when she could hope to finish it.

For Minnie it was even more bitter. If she had not been pregnant with Minnie, Alta McKay might have been able to finish *White Goddess* before the Crash, and she forever blamed Minnie for that first failure, which had marked the turning of the tide. Despised, Minnie put on pallid dresses and languished at the windows of that Spanish stucco heap, destined to stay with Alta McKay until she was released by marriage or unexpected riches, both possibilities which grew fainter with every passing year.

Some time in their twentieth year on the island, Kimu had made a flag of an old tarpaulin and hoisted it on a palm tree on the far side, where the others could not see it; if the enemy was going to find them he hoped it would be soon because the others were officers and could talk among themselves, but he was about to die of loneliness.

He was, through no effort of his own, more or less a recluse: Ethan Frome after the sled crashed, although he would not have known the allusion. He lived in an isolated farm house with his ailing wife, Sarah, and Essie, her ailing sister, and he had to take long walks to escape their voices, which filled the house and twined about his bones. He would walk the fences for hours and then come back to spend more time than he needed to fooling with the livestock in the barn. The winters had always been the worst, he had to be indoors more, and the windows would be sealed tight, enclosing the women's voices so that they seemed to be talking even when they weren't talking; he would have to clamp his hands over his ears and pray for spring, comforting himself with the thought that perhaps this spring he would be able to sell the farm, he could set his women up in a rest home and go to some place where it was always quiet. Before he could sell it, he would have to bring it up, and he didn't have the money to bring it up; he knew, further, that if he did have the money it would mean taking on some help and the help would want to talk to him the whole time he was in the fields, even as the women talked to him the whole time he was in the house, and he would never have any peace. He had managed to get along so far, feeding on the silence of the night, fleeing the women's voices in the silence of the fields, but this spring was filled with new menace: although she never did a lick of work around the house, his sister-in-law Essie was improved. She liked to go for little walks now, coming up behind him unexpect- edly in the barn, following him on his retreat to the fields. When he was too sorely pressed he would have to climb to the top of the last bales of hay in the loft and fall to brooding; if he had a buyer he would sell this place and put his women away and then buy a farm on the side of a mountain, where he could till the rocks in perfect solitude.

When a bystander stepped forward and said to Japheth, "You must be out of your mind," he said, "You may be right," and he and the others went on building the Ark as they had been told.

During one very bad period, partly to pass the time and partly to take their minds off their penetrating hunger, Shigamitsu had his men tell their life stories.

"I was at the head of my class," said Yoshi, although it was not precisely true. They had finished the captain's mango stew and the next to last tin of meat. The other one remained in the supplies cache underneath a pile of rocks and protective palm fronds, and although it was nowhere in sight it preyed on Yoshi's mind. "I was to go to the university to become an engineer. Then the war came and I can only hope that they will permit me to study for the university once again." He brightened. "Perhaps they will admit me without examinations, because of my great service to the Imperial Army of Japan."

"Perhaps there is no more university," said Captain Shigamitsu, who had secret misgivings; if all were well at home, why was the war still going on? He saw Yoshi's face blurring with anxiety and he went on quickly, "I mean, not as we know it. There will be more scientific methods, we will learn by injection, or by listening in our sleep."

"When I am an engineer," said Yoshi, "I shall have three houses." He was still thinking about the tin of meat. It was the last, and he couldn't stop thinking about it. "I shall sleep in one, I shall have all my women in another and love some and commit sins among the others whenever I care to, and in my third house . . ." His eyes glazed momentarily. "In the third I shall eat and eat and eat." If they opened the tin and ate it now, it would be all over with and he wouldn't have to go on thinking about it. But the captain would insist that they save it for another day.

"Not I," said Kimu, surprised at his own audacity. "I shall go back to Benji in our one house and we shall sleep and eat and breathe together, joined as one."

"Bless you," the captain said. He would have liked to know Kimu better, but with the situation as it was, it was impossible; he was the commanding officer, he understood Yoshi's ambitions and knew that his subordinates must be kept at the appropriate levels; at all costs, discipline would be maintained. Perhaps when they were all civilians together, in some future as yet unconceived . . .

"I shall design a new bridge, it will go all the way across Yokohama Bay." Yoshi looked at the others, thinking secretly: And you shall have to pay to go on it.

"There is nothing much to tell," said the captain, when it came his turn to attempt his life story. Indeed, there was not. His life had been so undistinguished before and they had been here for so long that it was hard for him to remember what had gone on. He offered, "I remember, I was very happy as a child." He wished now only for certain of his scrolls, for the collection of sharp knives he liked to use in cooking, for the variety of vegetables he would have found in the markets at home.

"Of course when we go home we will be heroes," Yoshi said.

They slept well that night despite their hunger; rather, two of them did. Yoshi was kept awake by the hunger which griped at his stomach, and although he tried every way he knew to deal with it, he understood finally that he was going to have to dig out that last tin of meat and get it over with for once and all.

He would have killed the captain to spare himself the shame, but there was no way; one minute he was crouched, bolting down the meat too fast to taste it, and in the next he looked up to find Shigamitsu standing over him with a look of great sadness, offering his sword. Although humiliation overcame him, Yoshi could not stop himself from licking the last fragment of meat off the raw edge of the tin and then he stood, knowing at once that his commanding officer was offering him the only honorable way out; he was to save face by using the ceremonial sword. The captain held out the sword for several seconds before Yoshi took it; then he turned with great gravity and left Yoshi alone.

But Yoshi could not do it. When dawn came Captain Shigamitsu would return to find him still sitting, contemplating the sword, and with a great sign of sadness he would take it from him, so removing the immediate command to do what was expected. Yoshi slunk off and was gone for three days. When he returned the captain was happy enough to have someone to share his cooking, because, pleasant as he was, the private had no appreciation of the subtler possibilities of taste, and for all his good will he had never been able to play a decent game of GO. By that time the private had killed rather a large iguana and, for the time being, they were able to set their difficulties aside; it was tacitly agreed that they would forget Yoshi's disgrace.

The effort of keeping her face muscles taut and her bosom at a certain elevation had begun to tell on Alta McKay. She ran the film twice a day now, rushing from screen to dressing-room mirror with an urgency that troubled her, and when Minnie would try to follow, she would turn on her, snapping: "Why don't you go out for a change? Why don't you ever have any friends?"

There was no answer Minnie could give. She had grown so accustomed to life in the house that she could not get along outside it; if she ate anywhere else she was acutely conscious of people watching her chew each bite, waiting for her to swallow, and so her mouth would dry out and the food would lodge there, sometimes she thought forever; if she tried to talk to somebody outside the house her head would bob and her hands tremble beyond her control, her voice would fail and her throat tighten in an orgy of self-consciousness, so that she chose to stay in the house until the day when Alta, maddened by her daughter's failings, jammed a twenty-dollar bill into her purse and pushed her out the door, saying, "I want you to go downtown and don't come back until you've had some fun."

Minnie gasped and unfocused her eyes, waggling her hands against the brightness of the sun. Given her choice she would have gone back inside at once but she was conscious of Alta in the Moorish tile archway, watching to be sure she did not falter.

Minnie took the bus that ran by the end of the long drive and spent the rest of the day in cheap department stores, buying a lipstick and a bright print dress and a pair of sandals, all from counters holding distressed merchandise. Then, tremulous with haste, she ducked into a ladies' room and put them on, impulsively stuffing her old clothes into the paper-towel bin. When she went out she was conscious of a change in herself and the way people looked at her; she squared her shoulders and for once found it easy to smile, mingling with crowds so dense that they dizzied her. She had gone no more than a block when she grew faint, welcoming the gathering darkness with the lunatic thought that she would be perfectly happy if she could die here and never go back, knowing instinctively that it would never work that way for her.

She could not know that despite her age she looked young and vulnerable, limply pretty, sagging against a revolving door. She fell into a faint and woke to find herself supported by an extremely nice-looking man just about her age.

"I'm so sorry," she said.

"Nonsense, I'm happy to help." He was looking into her face as if hypnotized. "Funny, you look just like someone I know."

"Oh look," she said, "the door has dirtied your coat, and it's all my fault."

"My pleasure."

"Let me pay to have it cleaned."

"Oh don't worry about that," he said, "I've come into a bit of money recently. May I take you home?"

"Oh yes, thank you," said Minnie. He was not handsome but he was *nice*, he was old enough for it to be sensible for her to fall in love with him and what's more he seemed drawn to her, holding her gently by one elbow and bending as if to protect her from whatever came.

"Yes," he said, although she would not have brought it up again, "I've come into a little money. As a matter of fact, I'm looking for someplace to invest. Who *is* it you remind me of?" He was staring fixedly into her face.

"Perhaps you've heard of my mother," she said, and told him, just as they came up the drive.

"Of course, I've seen all her movies." His eyes were shining. "But you're even prettier."

"She'll be very happy to meet you," Minnie said. She could see Alta McKay stirring just beyond the beads which covered the glass arches in the door.

"Damn fool music, damn fool kids, why would I want to do a thing like that?"

"They'll pay you a fortune," the real estate broker said.

And so he had a chance to sell his farm to a rock festival promoter. He had two weeks in which to think it over, two weeks to break the news to his womenfolk and make arrangements for them at the nursing home, then he could cut out like a bird set free, he would never have to listen to either of them again. He held his secret, coddling it in his bosom, feeding on it in an orgy of silence, aware that once he made the deal and set the machinery in process it would be irrevocable, and he would have to do a lot of talking before he finally got shut of it all.

Despite all of Alta McKay's anxiety and her insistence on showing *White Goddess* each time he came, her daughter's romance flowered, with this quiet, self-effacing rich man presenting himself at the mansion each night, proposing at last in the stillness of each early morning, accepting Minnie's explanation that she could not leave the house until *White Goddess* was finished and she was free; he may not have understood that Minnie was, as well, frightened at the prospect of leaving this house where she had been safe for so long.

So it happened that he came in one night with a lawyer and a plan;

they would finish *White Goddess,* fulfilling all their hopes and leaving them free to begin again; he put it to them both, to Minnie, who was loving but uncertain, to Alta, who may have known that she would at last be forced to look at the screen and see her own true and present face, that even with the movie finished, parts of it would never please her, it could never measure up to the picture she had in her mind any more than LaMont could match her memories; he probably never loved her anyway, nor could she be sure she would love LaMont . . .

"It's an offer," he said. Essie had followed him to the barn. "They want me to sell the farm."

"You can't do that," she said, and, abruptly, twined her arms around him as surely as if she had been thinking about it for months. Her arms were warm but frail; he could still step away.

Even if they had wanted it they could never have been delivered from the Ark because, as much as they railed against the closeness and the smell, they would have sailed on dutifully because with each choice the options grow more limited, no matter what people pretend, and by that time in their passage, deliverance was not one of the patterns; besides, it was going to take all the guts they had just to get off when they were supposed to, after the rain stopped and the mountain emerged.

Although planes and carriers and escort ships were circling an area some hundred miles south of there, the space capsule splashed down in the waters just off their island, and after an intolerable wait, the astronaut emerged and swam to shore, stripped of his space suit but impressive in the white coverall with his name and the American flag stitched to the left breast.

As he came out of the water the Japanese backed into fighting formation, crouching and begging him to fight.

"Oh my God," the astronaut said, taking in the stick figures with rusted weapons, the tattered uniforms.

Somebody said, "Banzai."

But he only said, "Oh, you poor sons of bitches," and tried to explain. ". . . and we have television now," he finished, "and I just got back from the moon."

They shook their heads, still menacing.

"You don't understand," he said. "You're saved."

But they did; Shigamitsu was, in the end, happy enough on the island; he had often thought he would not care to go back to a homeland filled with uncertainties and surprises, any more than Yoshi would want to return in disgrace; Kimu was thinking, in panic, I am so old and thin now, she will not recognize me; they were all caught up in a vertiginous view of the future, if they were not careful it would snatch them up and sweep them away.

". . . do you understand?"

Shigamitsu had English, so he had received the message a little faster than the others, and had been able to consider for a moment before he passed it on, but there turned out to be no need for consultation; the others understood as well as he and their wills were already forming, as a pearl will form itself around a grain of sand, enclosing their safe, vestigial lives; without a word they all three raised their rifles and shot the interloper dead.

"A Yankee trick," said Yoshi, because they had to say something.

"Yes," said Captain Shigamitsu, and they resumed their game of GO.

Great Escape Tours Inc.

Day after day, the folks who couldn't get up the scratch for the trip would sit around under the trees in Williams Park in St. Petersburg, Florida, and speculate the whole time the others were gone. It wasn't that they wished the rich tourists ill, exactly, just because some people had the money for that kind of foolishness while other people had to scrounge along on Social Security and bitty little checks from the kids; it was just that it pained the hell out of them to see the idle rich going into the kiosk day after day just because they happened to be able to afford it. What pained Dan Radford and his friends most, though, was to see the chosen few going off on GREAT ESCAPE TOURS INC. and then, by God, coming *back*.

"Damn fools," Dan would say, clattering his teeth in rage, "you'd think once they got where they're going, they'd have the good sense to stay there."

His wife Theda always tried to calm him, saying, "Maybe there are reasons that they can't."

"So what?" Dan would press his lips together, irritated because his new teeth had never fit right, not in all the years he had owned them. "I'll tell you one thing, Theda, if I ever get on one of those tours, they'll whistle in hell before I come back."

All the old gang felt the way Dan did; the whole thing held a morbid fascination, and they used to rally every morning, often skipping breakfast to get down to the kiosk before the neon sign went on. They would gather on the semicircle of benches and watch the sign flashing in three different colors: GREAT ESCAPES, INC. They all knew each other pretty well by this time; there they sat, the old gang: the Radfords, Hickey Washburn in his sun visor and string shirt, Big Marge, Tim and Patsy O'Neill, who, at eighty-two, still held hands wherever they went; that noted man about town and witty gigolo in the black-and-white spectators, Iggy the Rake. They came from the boarding-houses and cheap hotels near Mirror Lake, muttering hellos in the early morning light, and, without fail, taking exactly the same place on the benches every day. From time to time Iggy would bring a girl, some chipper septuagenarian he'd had his eye on, but the rest of them tolerated that because Iggy was notoriously fickle and, whoever she was, she wouldn't last long. Occasionally some misguided outsider would sit down, all innocence, but there would be such a harrumphing, such a rattle of morning papers and pointed clearing of throats that nobody made the mistake more than once.

It was important to get there before the first tourist came, so they could count them as they went into the kiosk; they had to be able to check them off accurately when they returned late that afternoon, and the old gang wanted a fairly close description of each so that, when the tour ended and they all filed out, they could look for possible changes wrought by the trip. The gang all brought their lunches in string bags or brown paper sacks but usually they would begin nibbling around nine, out of sheer nervousness, and by the time the flashing light on top of the kiosk signalled departure time, at ten, they would have eaten their entire lunches in a fit of frustration, and so they would be left with laps full of crumbs and sandwich papers, with nothing much to do but brush themselves off and wait for the 2 P.M. band concert, which might be cancelled if it rained.

By five, when the tours returned, they were usually wild; they would have spent the dreariest part of the afternoon talking about what the rich tourists were probably doing this very moment, where they were and what it was like, how *they* would certainly never come back, the way these suckers did. Since rumor had it that once you got there, wherever it was, you were *young,* none of the old gang could figure out exactly why these people always came back, why they didn't look any different, or why, when the old gang would get one aside and try to pump him, they got no answer at all, or worse than no answer. It made Theda think of the time she got her sister Rhea alone, right after Rhea's honeymoon; Theda was wild, pressing her: *What was it like?* and Rhea either tried hard to tell her and couldn't, or else she tried hard to look as if she was trying to answer and couldn't find any real way to explain. Pressed, the richly dressed men and women coming out of the kiosk at the end of the day would turn to the old gang with some of the same mixed motives, spreading their hands helplessly and saying, "What can we say?"

Because she found it hard to think about where they went on the GREAT ESCAPE TOURS INC. or what they were doing while they were away, Theda always dwelled on the clothes the women were wearing: aqua, mostly, or pink, because it "did things" for their withered complexions; to a woman they had silverblue hair, and no matter how hot it got or how hot it was going to be where they were going, they all wore silverblue mink stoles. She resented the mink and the diamonds and the silver or gold kid wedgies, she resented the fact that she and Dan had worked hard all their lives and had come to this: a bench in St. Petersburg, Florida, with a rather pleasant room in a house that wasn't theirs, and children who never, ever came to visit. They couldn't even afford a car. It had all sounded good enough to them when they were back home in snowy Boise, planning their future, but of course they had reckoned without being stuck down there summer *and* winter, and they had thought Dan's checks were going to go farther than they did, and what's more they hadn't either of them expected to feel so confounded *old*.

She didn't mind for herself so much as for Dan; she hated to lie in bed listening to his breath rattle, she hated the half hour he had to spend in the bathroom every morning, coughing and hawking, before he was ready to face the day; she hated to watch his failing step, and most of all she hated the way his face and his chest caved in because she could remember when he was square-faced and full-muscled, and she could never be sure exactly when he had started to sink in on himself, or when his hands had begun to tremble, nor did she remember exactly when it was that he had waked her in the night for the first time, crying, "Mama," out of his restless sleep.

They claimed GREAT ESCAPE TOURS INC. took you to a place where you were young. There must be something the matter with it, because nobody seemed to want to stay, but if Dan wanted to go there, wherever it was, then she wanted to go too, and as she watched him totter around the kiosk this particular morning she realized that if they were going, it had better be sooner rather than later, because he was getting crosser and shakier all the time now, and she herself had begun to wake in the nights with an uneasy, dizzy feeling, as if it was all just about to drop out from under her, so she had to wonder just how much time either of them had left.

Which meant that when he came back from his morning circuit of the kiosk this particular day, and said, "I think we can do it," and Iggy and the others gathered around to listen to his plan, Theda knew she was going to go along with it.

Iggy was going to be the inside man, and all the others had some part, large or small, in the master plan. Once Iggy's new rich girl-friend paid his way inside, Hickey Washburn would create a diversion by pretending a heart attack in the dirt outside the kiosk. When the attendant rushed outside to tend to Hickey, the O'Neills would rush him, snaring his head in Patsy's shopping bag while Big Marge held his hands behind him and the Radfords tied them with Theda's blue bandanna. Then Iggy would open the door from inside, and after that . . .

"Yeah," Patsy O'Neill said, "what happens after that?"

Dan shrugged, more or less at a loss. "I guess we'll have to play it by ear."

The first problem was Iggy's rich girlfriend; they had to find one, so between nine and five they began to wander afield, stalking the precincts of the Soreno and the Vinoy Park and going as far as the new downtown Hilton. When they thought they had found the right girl, Iggy sidled up and sat down next to her on the bench, while the others moved back to an inconspicuous distance and cheered him on. They had pooled their entertainment money for the next month so Iggy could take her out to dinner, and by the time Iggy was ready to take her dancing, Hickey Washburn was so committed to the plan that he sacrificed a yellowing dinner jacket from his salad days, and Tim O'Neill proffered, with shaking hands, a set of diamond studs which looked as if they had never been removed from their treasure box of aged, cracking leatherette. Although they all had respect for Iggy's "line," Theda and Patsy had further advice for Iggy when he got his girl alone; they all threw themselves into it, all except for Big Marge, who seemed unaccountably sullen and wouldn't even come down to the park to see Iggy off on his big date.

After Patsy kissed him on the cheek and Theda slipped a red carnation in his buttonhole, the boys walked Iggy down to the convertible he had hired for the occasion, and then they came back and the whole gang (except for Marge) sat around in the park and talked until it got dark. Memories flicked on and off like fireflies and they found themselves alternately sad, at what they would be leaving behind for GREAT ESCAPE TOURS INC., and tremulous, because they could not be certain what they would find once they got there, wherever it was. They speculated hotly about what Iggy and his girl were doing now, and the rest of the time they were reminiscent, valedictory, awash in nostalgia for things they had never even had, and by the time they got up to go, their old bones were stiff and some of their joints had locked, so that Patsy had to help Tim up and Theda had to thump Hickey Washburn on the back two or three times to get him going.

They knew they ought to be home getting their beauty sleep, resting up for the big trip, but they lingered on the sidewalk outside the park until Dan said, firmly, "Well, tomorrow's the big day," and they all nodded because, without having any real reason to believe it, they all thought it was.

As it turned out, it was. Iggy had scored in the convertible on some moonlit strand, using a combination of sweet talk and adept fumbling at the lady's neck which served to remind her of things they were both more or less beyond, telling her they would be realized in the grass the minute she paid his way on GREAT ESCAPE TOURS INC. When he got home from his date he was so excited that he called everybody and told them all about it even though it was the middle of the night. The only one who was asleep, or pretended to be asleep, when he called was Big Marge, who yawned heavily into the telephone and said she guessed she would be there in the morning, yes she remembered her instructions. She never once asked if he had a good time on his date.

None of them slept that night; instead they lay awake in the moonlight, dreaming, planning or scheming: Big Marge flexed her body in the trough of her bedsprings and vowed to get rid of Iggy's girl first thing, so she could have him for herself. She would make him crawl first, and then she would forgive him and love him forever. She thought of the place as a mirror world: they would all run around in the negative, with faces dark and the shadows blanched and their feet barely touching the ground. Hickey Washburn lay in his rented room and thought about being twenty-one, which he was sure was how old he would always be in the new place. He couldn't quite remember what it had been like but he thought he could handle it. The O'Neills touched bony hands across the gulf between their cheap twin beds; he was thinking that if everybody was young where they were going, maybe he and Patsy would go back to a point before they were even married; then he could take a close look at her and all the other young chickies who would be there, rosy and bouncing, and make a leisurely choice. Iggy was thinking about all the girls too, but his thoughts were somewhat more specific. Listening to Dan cough, Theda lay as still as she could, holding her breath lest she jiggle him and make it worse. She knew they had to get there, one way or another; she might even have to drag him the last part of the way, and she summoned all her strength, already wondering if they could make it.

As it turned out, Dan rose with a preternatural energy even before it got light, pulling Theda into his feverish preparations. They both had to bathe and dress as carefully as if they were going to be presented to some queen or other, and Dan sat on the edge of the bed and fidgeted while Theda tried on dress after dress at his request, settling at last on the pretty lavender voile that was the same color as the dress she had been wearing when he met her for the first time. They got down to the park too early, but so had everybody else; Big Marge was slumped in her usual place with a string bag between her feet, and when Theda asked her what was in it she snatched it away and wouldn't answer. The O'Neills had eaten all their sandwiches in their anxiety and Hickey Washburn was pacing back and forth as if he had forgotten something and was trying with all his might to bring it back. They were all too restless to sit quietly, and so by the time the church clock struck eight they were keyed tight and jerking like marionettes and by the time it struck nine and the lighted sign went on above the kiosk: GREAT ESCAPES INC., they were all slumped on the benches again like tired children, testy and spent, and when Iggy appeared with his rich new girlfriend, they could barely acknowledge his conspiratorial nod. They may have been put off by his new girl's obvious riches: the white mink stole over the pink playsuit, the shoes with the Lucite platforms, the platinum-blonde wig made out of real hair, or it may have been the way Iggy looked, dapper and fresh, so sure of himself that he had slept all night instead of tossing anxiously. He seemed to sense their difficulty and so he excused himself from his girl and came over, dropping little pills into everybody's hands and saying, "Chew these."

Theda said, "What's this?"

"Never mind," Iggy said hastily. "It'll give you a lift."

"How do we know?" Tim O'Neill asked.

Iggy winked and wriggled his shoulders. "It works for me."

So they all popped the pills, whatever they were: Hickey Washburn was convinced they were goat glands, and began snorting and stamping; they tasted like Aspergum to the O'Neills and Feenamint to the Radfords and Big Marge took them for Benzedrine. It didn't matter what they were because they achieved the purpose: everybody galvanized and rushed the kiosk right on schedule, kicking out the enraged paying customers and the tour guide himself and locking the doors. They strapped themselves in the plush seats and heard the machinery start to whirl, carrying them off just as sirens and voices rose outside and the first policeman began battering the locked doors with his stick.

"And now, over the rooftops, through the corridors of time, for a unique and never-to-be-forgotten experience. Welcome to your Great Escape."

Whirling in darkness, Theda fixed on the unctuous recorded voice, reassured by memories of the 1939 World's Fair, when she had been pulled along in a comfy plush chair, listening to a voice that sounded like this one. She remembered she could hardly wait until 1942, and now . . .

". . . your tour guide will explain the limitations on arrival," the voice was saying, and Theda remembered with a pang of guilt that Dan had hit the tour guide on the head with something just before he pushed him outside and slammed the doors. Well, Iggy was a man of the world and so was Dan, so they should be able to make their way without too much trouble, and if they decided to stay wherever it was they were going, there would be no group leader to force them to return.

The voice was concluding, ". . . on the jungle gym at 4:55 P.M. to make the speedy and safe return. A bell will ring in case you can't tell time."

"What? Helpimfalling . . . UMP."

Theda was sitting on the ground blinking in the fresh sunlight, she had fallen off and landed on her hands and knees and now she was sitting in the dirt, her underpants were dirty and she had skinned her knees again and she knew her mommy would spank her the minute she got home because her brand-new dress was filthy dirty, and she was too big to cry but she felt so awful she started crying anyway.

"Sissy, sissy." He was hanging upside down from the jungle gym with his face right in front of her and she thought he ought to be a lot nicer to her but she couldn't remember why until she saw the way his nose had the big wart on it and his mouth went in a wavy line; then he yelled "Sissy, sissy," and she figured out that meant he really liked her or else he wouldn't be teasing her so she yanked on his arm and pulled him into the dirt next to her and while they were rolling around she figured it all out, saying, "Dan? Is that you, Dan?"

He squinted into her face. "Theda? What happened?"

She stood up, brushing off her dress and looking around at the other kids, who either swung furiously on the jungle gym or else sat in the dirt and cried. That one with the fat tummy must be Big Marge and the one in the baseball hat was probably Hickey Washburn, she would have to ask the other kids which ones were which because whatever they used to look like, before they got into that thing and took the trip, they didn't look like it anymore, they were all kids together, and she thought maybe it wouldn't be so bad after all because they could grow up together, and after they grew up they would be young men and women, strong, healthy, and she would never again have to wake up and listen to Dan coughing his blood out in the middle of the night.

She said, "Dan, I think we're here."

The one that was probably Iggy's girlfriend was doing cartwheels, but Iggy himself sat quietly in the dirt, feeling himself all over: face, arms, groin—groin! He stood up, comprehending, and came running. "This is awful. What are we going to do?"

They wanted to make the other kids get together and talk about it, but Timmy O'Neill was chasing Iggy's girlfriend around and Patsy and Hickey Washburn were fighting about Hickey's hat, everybody was screaming and yelling and the only people that would pay attention to Theda were Danny, because he liked her, and Iggy, who for one reason or another still had his moustache even though they were, every one of them, only six years old. There was a board screwed on the jungle gym with a whole bunch of rules written on it, but even though Theda had been quick at learning to read she couldn't figure it out. They were in a playground but they couldn't see any school, only a lot of grass all around, and she was already scared to go outside the fence and look around because they might get lost and besides, nobody knew what was out there, lions or tigers or ugly men that would offer them candy and drag them away.

Iggy climbed way up to the top of the jungle gym and looked all around. "Hey," he said, "what if this is all there is?"

"When we grow up we can be cowboys." Dan couldn't stop picking his nose. "And Theda can be the cowgirl."

Theda knew she ought to be thinking up things to do but she couldn't keep her mind on it, she felt so good she started running around and around the jungle gym and pretty soon Danny was chasing her and Iggy was chasing him, they all ran around and around, laughing and yelling until Big Marge tackled Iggy and they all fell down. She and Danny were wrestling, rolling over and over, he was sitting on her chest and holding her wrists down with his hands, she looked up into his face and thought, *Oh Dan,* but she didn't know where all the feelings came from or what they were, except that the main one was very, very sad.

Somebody started teasing Big Marge, they all called her Fatty now, she had this funny string bag she had brought with her and Hickey got it away from her and it turned out there was a gun inside, they were all scared to death of it so they dug a hole and buried it over by the swings. They played for a long long time, they played and played until Patsy O'Neill fell over a stick and skinned her knees and started to cry, and then Hickey got tired of sliding and Big Marge started crying for no reason and finally Iggy's girlfriend came out and said it, she sat down plump in the middle of the dirt and said:

"I'm hungry."

Everybody said, "Me too," but when they looked around for their lunchboxes there weren't any and there weren't any fruit trees around, they couldn't even find any dandelion stems, there was a water fountain and that was all, there might be a store out there somewhere but nobody had any allowance and besides, they were scared to go outside the fence and see, somebody might come to the playground looking for them and they wouldn't be there, or else they might get lost and never find their way back to the jungle gym, and the teacher had said they had better be on the jungle gym by five o'clock or else. They tried not to talk about hot dogs and everything, they all drank lots of water and tried to play some more, but they had run out of games to play and besides, people kept crying for no reason and finally Iggy said:

"This is no fun."

The others began, one by one: "I'm tired."

"I'm hungry."

"I'm bored."

"I'm *hungry.*"

Then Theda said it right out, "I want to go home." She was sitting on one end of the seesaw and Danny was on the other end, he got off his end so she went bump on the ground and he said,

"I'm not ever going home."

Theda said, "What if you don't get any supper?"

"I don't care."

Parts of Theda still remembered. "What if you have to stay like this?"

He set his feet wide in the dirt and stuck his chin out. "I don't care." Then he seemed to remember too, he said, "I hate it back there."

"What if it thunders? What if it rains?"

Dan said, "I don't care."

"Who's going to take care of you?"

He shrugged and got back on the other end of the seesaw. They sat there for a long long time, just sort of balancing, she didn't know how long it was but the light was getting different, the way it did when it was about time for you to say goodbye to all the other kids and go home to your nice warm supper, everybody had stopped playing together and they were all off pretending to do things by themselves, humming on the swings or digging in the dirt or singing some song with a thousand million verses, putting sticks in piles and then knocking them over, and waiting.

Finally the bell rang. Everybody on the playground got up from what they were doing, Theda got off the seesaw without even looking and they all ran for the jungle gym, they were all climbing up, they heard somebody that sounded like all their mothers saying:

SUPPERTIME.

It made Theda feel good thinking about it, she would go home and have chicken soup and then get in her bed with her brand-new Billy Whiskers book and at seven aclock Mommy would kiss her good night, she would go back to the guest house and after supper she would watch the early movie on TV in their room, and Dan would kiss her good night, he would start coughing . . .

Dan.

She looked all over for him and saw that he wasn't on the jungle gym, he was way over there on the other side of the playground, standing up there in the middle of the teeter-totter, with one foot on either side of the axis, balancing. He might not remember why he wasn't coming back with her but he wasn't coming back, he would rather stay here and starve to death if he had to, he would stay six years old forever, just so he wouldn't have to go back to his old self in his old age, and the more she thought about it the more she knew she ought to leave him, if she went home she would die soon which would be fine with her, but she couldn't leave him, that was *Dan*, and she had to . . .

She jumped off just before the second bell rang. She landed on her hands and knees again, she had opened up the skinned places and her dress was really dirty now, but she wasn't ever going home so it probably didn't matter, but when she sat up and looked at the jungle gym she wanted to cry because all the kids were gone now, everybody was gone except that kid over there on the seesaw, Danny, he wasn't always nice to her but he was her best friend so she got up and went over to where he was still balancing and pretending not to notice her.

After a while he looked down after all so she said, "Want to play?"

He jumped down. "What do you want to do?"

She was looking at the playground gates now, it looked like there was just grass out there, maybe it was grass all the way to the edge and you could fall off, or else something would get you, but she knew she and Danny couldn't stay here because somebody might come and drag them home, so she started for the gate, trying to be brave.

"Let's go see."

Love Story

I have brought this on myself. It would be easy enough for me to lie back and say Oh, fate, or Oh, the perfidy, and blame her for my undoing, instead of laying it all to my love for her, but I have always been honest with myself, and if I am brought low now it is not because she led me on; she gave me not one moment of encouragement, she barely gave me a smile, and if she smiled at all it was not because of what I was but, rather, what she thought I was. If I am alone in jail now it is because of my own petty foolishness. I have only myself to blame.

Of course I am not the first nor will I by any means be the last male to be done in by his love for a member of the fair sex, and I take some comfort in that; it puts me at one with the rest of humanity, in an emotional proximity which I had always assumed but had so lately and so sadly come to doubt.

Perhaps we all assume we have more in common with our fellows than we could ever have; we need to think we are all more or less alike, and I can only hope for the rest of you that you shall never, ever have to experience a disillusionment as sudden and painful as mine.

I have always lived among people, first in the village, where there were brown families coming and going and the children would come into the banana groves to look for me, and later in the most similar and compatible circumstances I could find. When I came to the city I was fortunate to find lodgings in a place where there were plenty of plants for me to hide among, and the air was always warm and moist. There was always water running and there was always plenty to eat: sandwiches and marzipan sweets, biscuits and cakes moistened with tea. All my afternoons were enlivened by music, and until this last week I could always creep out of hiding to watch the ladies in their tea gowns, coming and going in elegance and grace.

Nobody asked me to leave the safety and pleasure of the Palm Court, but on that certain fateful day I was drawn, driven by inner compulsions which would brook no denial, and, having exposed myself, I must take the consequences, more: having done wrong, I must accept the punishment for that wrong. I have been expelled from paradise, and rightly so.

Perhaps if I had been more beautiful by human standards. Perhaps if she had made a greater attempt to understand me. Shall I blame it all on fate, or circumstance?

I am a prime male of my species; why could she not accept me for what I was? I have glossy black hair all over my body, and all my legs are made elegant by skirts or chaps of black hair. Once I saw a woman in a monkey-fur coat and I thought: *You would be proud to own such a coat as I have, you would not have to take it off at night;* she neither saw nor heard, but only passed me by. Even here in prison, people come to see me and admire. "My God," they say. "Those eyes (are those the eyes?)." Or, "Great heavens, he has a body the size of your fist."

And so I do. I am vigorous, I am still young, I am extremely handsome; I have always been so handsome by my own standards that it never occurred to me to say that I was not handsome by human standards, and I wonder now whether she turned on me for that, or rather because I presumed too much. It might be safe to say even now that, taken absolutely, I am most gorgeous, and her revulsion, the pernicious fear and its concomitant results were rather the effluvia of a deranged mind; if I had been Cary Grant she might have responded that way all the same.

You may wonder why I ever chose to leave the rain forest. If I had remained there, king in my own habitat, I would have come to the appropriate fulfillment, beautiful in a place which could appreciate my beauty.

I must confess I did not leave by choice. I was living happily in my clump of bananas, when, before I could make out what was happening, the world as I knew it came to an abrupt end. There were heavy crashing sounds in the underbrush, gruff voices and sickening chopping sounds. I could hear the banana plants cry out; I could smell their white blood, but before I could find out what was happening, much less try to take some action, the clump in which I was living was suddenly upended and I had to cling for purchase, going along in a near swoon to heaven only knew what terrible destiny. My clump was thrown, bananas and all, into a cart which began a nightmarish journey which I do not wish to recount. Then the auction: slavery. Then the boat. I think we must all have been in some kind of cold storage, the bananas and I; I cried out time after time, hoping to hear some response which could indicate to me that there were others like me aboard, but all the air gave back to me was night and silence, the shouts of the deckhands, the banana branches' dying moans.

At last, perhaps only to survive, I fell into a faint or swoon, and I do not remember another thing until I came to myself in the elevator, rising to the roof of a very old and famous hotel in what I now know to be New York City.

I must explain that at the time I could not have identified the service elevator, but I lived blissfully in the Plaza for several months before I fell on evil fortune, and in that time I learned a great deal about Room Service and Front, the *haut monde* and even *la vie bohème.*

When I first reached the roof, however, there was every likelihood that I would never leave it. I could smell gorilla the minute the doors slid open and the service cart bearing my bunch of bananas was rolled out onto the roof. There were dozens of men, blinding lights and the flash of an occasional photographic bulb. I could hear the television announcer, and although I had not yet picked up the language, the import of his speech was plain:

Here was the first (or largest/or meanest) gorilla ever brought back from somewhere or other, and over there (I could see between two bananas) was the explorer who had brought him back, and after he was photographed just once more he was going to eat this bunch of bananas (and me along with it) for the cameras, and after that they were probably going to take him back down in the elevator and put him in an open-topped convertible for the inevitable ticker-tape parade.

I quailed in my bananas. I could hope to make my escape from the maw of the gorilla, but even if I did, one of those dozens of bystanders would see me; there would be screams and screeches, not because I am not handsome, but because people are unpredictable and intolerant; they would find me so—unexpected, and somebody would be bound to take off after me with a window pole, or try to smash me with his shoe.

Just then fate did me an enormous favor. There was a woman standing near me, limp-waisted and beautiful in what I now know to be a ranch mink stole. She was, apparently, the explorer's light of love, and she was also quite obviously bored with the proceedings. I should imagine she had just said, Honestly, Harry, you love that gorilla more than you do me.

Whatever she said, she was in an obvious rage, and before any of us could apprehend her intent or attempt to stop her, she had slapped the explorer and turned on her heel, pushing the elevator button and waiting impatiently for it to come. Of course the explorer was upset, the gorilla was upset, and in the flurry in which they prodded and shot flash bulbs at the gorilla to keep him from attacking the young lady and so avenging the affront to his beloved Harry, I leaped from my cover in the bananas and nestled in the folds of her furry stole, taking a strange and perhaps forbidden comfort from the body warmth which came to me through the folds of her cashmere coat.

I could not have chosen a more fortunate expedient. She went into the elevator just as the gorilla lunged for both of us; the sliding doors closed, just missing its fingers, and the two of us were safe. As we descended, I could hear her cursing and muttering under her breath, and I can only assume she was promising herself some kind of consolation the minute we got to the main floor, because, after a certain amount of unpleasant jouncing down plushly carpeted corridors, we came at least to what I then considered to be the Kingdom of Heaven. There were soft lights, there was music playing, there was perfume in the air and there would be, that afternoon and for months thereafter, delectable things to eat, so that there was no element to indicate that it was not in fact a kind of paradise; only later did I learn that it was called the Palm Court, in the Plaza Hotel.

Who would not give the sun and the moon to dwell in those marbled halls? Who would not bask in the rich atmosphere, the *embarras de richesses,* where every waiter is grander and more diffident that all of the guests? Who would not wish to live forever in peace and contentment in this earthly paradise for the very rich? Can I hope for you who have never lived there to understand that *noblesse oblige?* Can I convey to you the *cachet?* Or my *désespoir* at having to let it go?

Ah, well. Perhaps it was *hubris,* perhaps it was always destined to end the way it did. Perhaps my fate was written in the stars some centuries ago, along with Pliny's, and poor Caesar's, and even forwarned I would have found myself compelled to act it out to the bitter finish.

I only know she came in for the first time three weeks ago, she who was the key to my undoing even as she became my light of life. I was living happily in one of the palm-pots at the time, perfectly concealed by assorted ferns around the base. All at once I was knocked on all my heels by the most devastating scent I have ever experienced, but instead of having the wits to lie in the mulch, where all was dark and silent, simply letting the waves of scent wash over me, instead of lying low until the excitement passed, I had to put first one leg, then two, then three around the edge of the fern and poke my head out to have a look.

She was not just a woman, or just a beautiful woman, she was WOMAN; it was not enough that she had dark hair like spun jet, rising higher than the fountain; it was not enough that her dress was studded with black sequins and her shoulders draped in a black ostrich-feather boa. Oh, my lights and my stars, her *legs* were black: she had on black stockings which were fringed right down to the black buckles of her shoes. She was black, like me, she was shiny, like me, it was almost as if she knew I was there and had set out to dress for me; I have never been so moved.

I had by that time picked up enough of the language to be able to make out from the conversation of the others just who she was. She was a very great diva, an opera singer; the *maître d'* bent over her hand and called her "Madame." She spoke musically and constantly in the most exotic foreign language I had ever heard; I wanted to come out of hiding and follow her and bask in every word.

Drawn, hypnotized, I threw all caution to the winds and approached. I had to skin down the edge of the flowerpot, which I had not left for weeks, and make my cautious way across the carpet, thinking that perhaps even if I *were* seen, I would be taken for just another spot upon the rug. I made it to her table undetected, I scuttled under the cloth, and then, oh saints take me! Then I pressed myself against her shoe. She did not start or jump; I do not wish to believe she did not feel the ardent pressure of my body; I prefer to think she felt my presence and permitted it. Who is to say she did not lead me on?

When she left I was devastated, but I learned soon enough that she had come to us from Italy (I loved her, but would I ever be able to say *cara mia?*), and she was going to be a guest at our hotel.

I fed on her visits; I lived for them, spinning out hour after hour without even eating, bursting into life only when I heard her chattering in that wonderful tongue. Sometimes she only swept by without stopping, in haste to be on her way about town, but other times, oh, at least twice a week, she would come in for tea, and I thought at the time that this would be enough; I could live for her visits, stringing them out one from another in a web of love which would become a lasting tribute to both our lives; I suppose I thought we could go on like this forever; how could I hope to understand that life is brief and love, too cruel.

Still I dared not show myself to her, and I thought I would not need to; it was enough to be able to scuttle into a palm tree near her table when she came in. I could have lived the rest of my life that way, except that, just last week, I saw the *maître d'* look after the departing Madame with great sadness, saying: "Too bad. No more of those tips. By this time Friday she will be gone."

I had not yet worked out which days were Fridays and which were not, but I could tell from his tone that I did not have much more time. I would see her at least one last time; I could even try to express my love to her, but even then we would have only that one fleeting moment together, and she would be gone. I could not bear to think of it. She was all I had ever wanted in a woman, and Friday, whenever Friday came, she would be gone.

I laid my plans carefully. By this time she had a favorite table and a certain chair she liked to sit in when she came to tea, and so I stationed myself just underneath the seat, locating myself during the night when there was only the custodial staff to contend with, a few dim ladies with brooms who would not notice me except as one more dark spot on the rug. I climbed up to the underside of her seat, hanging doggedly in a sort of trance or semi-coma, prepared to hang upside down for days if necessary, to be wakened to life and action only by the sound of her voice.

I do not know how long I waited before she came. I must have waited until the fateful Friday, because when she did come in she looked dressed for a journey, and when the *maître d'* came to her she chattered in Italian and then her companion said, yes, as soon as she attended to a few things in her suite, Madame was leaving for Rome.

I swung under the seat, vertiginous, and finally, with the strength born of desperation, I made my move. First I pushed one leg out from under the seat, then another and then another, and then I was on the side of the seat, and then I was in her lap. Dear Heaven. I was afraid she would look down and see me, and then, in a few more quick, breathless moves, I was inside the wide sleeve of her black fur coat. Safe. When we got back to her room I would declare myself. Perhaps she would not feel love for me at first, but if she would at least tolerate, and begin to accept me, then I would be on the way: I could attach myself to her retinue, perhaps in the capacity of a re-tainer, and so, one way or another, I would be able to follow her to Rome. I did not think beyond that. If I could go to Rome with her then I could be with her always, and if I could be with her always, then I did not have to think beyond that.

It was a breathtaking ride down the corridor; Madame was in a rage for one reason or another, Madame strode, crying out a string of expletives as she moved. I had hoped to lie low until a more felicitous moment and then come out and make myself known, but she was in such a rage that when she reached the suite she ripped off the coat so that the sleeves came out inside out and so there I was on top, looking at her from the bed, and there she was, looking at me.

I had no choice but to come right out with it, and so I tried to tell her of my love.

I can only say "Tried." I do not wish to recount what happened next. Suffice it to say that she was so shocked as to forget her great beauty and the beauty of her nature; she was not the great lady I had thought her, for she used language I never hope to hear again; she was vicious, she was brutal, turning on me like a fishwife or a wrath-ful shrew; she was not even Italian. Oh the disillusionment when she began to curse and scream at me in the pedestrian language I heard in the Palm Court every day, and as she screamed she took after me and tried to hit me with her shoe.

So perhaps it was her fault after all. I turned on her in my rage and pain; I turned on her, not with any intention of defending myself, but because all my love had been hurled back at me and had turned in on itself, so that I was, rather, in an agony of fury. So I did what I had to; I bit her, and I am not sorry. Who would not have done the same?

The last I saw of her was as they moved her onto the stretcher; she was screaming a lot of things no lady ever says; being sensitive, I tried not to listen. I was already sick with remorse for acting against her, but she was already on the way out on the rolling stretcher, off to get de-toxified, the orderly said; the implications cut through me but there was neither time nor means for me to make amends.

Perhaps the keepers of this prison understand my remorse will trouble me far more than any punishment they could contrive; whatever their motives, they have left me more or less alone, tossing in pallid food pellets which are bitter travesties of the macaroons and *petits fours* I have grown accustomed to; no one ever stops in to ask me, Well, how goes it, or What's new with you.

Life does, however, have its consolations. I would gather that I have a certain amount of status in this prison. Just over the fence beyond my quarters is a plate glass window, and ever since I got here, people have been filing past that glass. I can imagine what they are saying: He's a big one, ain't he and, My God, he's got a body as big as your fist.

And so I do. It is not for mere show that they have put my name in black letters on a plaque just outside my nest. I have a name to be reckoned with, in the most elevated language of them all:

TARANTULA Tetrapneumones (Myglidae)

The Visible Partner

I do not like it here. It's damp and smelly and the chill is creeping up through my ankles and haunches and heading for my brain. If I don't get out I am going to catch my death in another minute but I am stuck here, crouching in the dark while that fool runs around naked which means I couldn't see him even if it was light enough. I don't even know where he is running around, who he is with. He could be a hundred miles from here, at my elbow, in my erstwhile office, going through my most private things.

An invisible man needs a visible partner, he said when he made the pitch. It sounded reasonable enough. Who knew I was going to be left holding the bag in a dozen different places, or that I would lose my job, my reputation, my girl, my last chance for a reasonable life? Who could foretell that the formula would make him crazier and crazier? I should have been more careful, I should have guessed he would be difficult to live with and impossible to get rid of, but he sold me such a bill of goods and besides, he said I would get to take turns.

That's exactly what he said. "And besides, we're going to take turns being invisible, you'll get to see what it's really like."

"What's it like, Ivor?"

There were ripples in the air where I think he was standing. There were sounds of him waving his arms and sighing all at the same time, he was communicating something mysterious and wonderful. "I can't explain, Sam, you'll have to feel it for yourself."

"In a pig's valise," I said. "I haven't even agreed to do it."

"OK, I'll take my business elsewhere."

"Wait a minute, friend, that's our formula you were fooling around with, it's just as much mine as yours."

"Our formula plus Ingredient X." He pulled something out and set it on the table. It was a tiny flask. "My invention." I made a grab for it but it had already disappeared: in his clenched fist? In a pocket? In his armpit? "You could spend the rest of your life looking for Ingredient X."

"All right, bastard, who needs it?"

"Think of the power." His voice was coming from a different corner of the room and no matter how fast I turned I couldn't follow. "You haven't lived until you've felt the warm air all over you, or run naked in a crowd."

"Naked? You're naked?"

"Stupid. Even socks would show up. I can be naked anywhere." He paused heavily. "Theatrical dressing rooms, girls' locker rooms, anyplace."

"Aren't you cold?"

"Idiot." He kicked over a chair. "Banal pedestrian idiot. I never should have wasted my time with you. I never should have . . ."

I could hear his voice retreating. "Wait a minute." Images were crowding in. I imagined myself invisible in a dozen different places, soft breezes on my bare ass. "Ivor, wait."

He sounded intolerably smug. "I knew you'd come around. Now get me something to put on."

"What's in it for me?"

"Fifty percent of the profits. Besides, I told you, you'll get your turn."

I got my hooded bathrobe and the slipper socks and a ski mask, he put them on and the only disconcerting parts were the gap at the throat and the great empty spaces visible through the eyeholes and the mouth. At least it made him a little easier to deal with, I knew where to look when we were talking and he couldn't sneak up on me.

I said, "OK, Ivor, what's the plan?"

"I thought we could push through your promotion."

All right, I jumped. "What do you know about that?"

"I've been hanging around the department tenure meetings," he said. "You're in big trouble, friend."

"How could you—" I could see scraps of nothing between my gloves and the bathrobe sleeves. "Oh, right."

In spite of the fact that I am a somewhat unorthodox chemist, and I have been known to spend valuable classroom time getting my students to work on commercial formulae, like cleaning fluids and aphrodisiacs, my case had been forwarded to the department, and now it was up or out. This was a sore point with Ivor, who was let go two days before he'd disappeared. The chairman had him in to break the news, he screamed, "You'll be sorry," and stormed out and simply disappeared. Nobody had seen or heard from him. Until he turned up in my library, that is. Hell yes I was surprised.

"What do you care whether I get tenure? I mean especially since you didn't."

"Let's say I have a vested interest. I need your lab. I can't refine my formula without proper equipment."

"Our formula," I reminded him.

"Tell that to the tenure committee and see how far it gets you. Do you want me to help you or not?"

"I don't know, I . . ."

"Your case looks pretty bad."

"All right, all right, what do you think you can do for me?"

"Well to begin with, I can replace a couple of letters in your dossier. To be frank, they couldn't be worse."

"And if I don't cooperate?"

"Slkkkk." He ran a gloved finger across his invisible throat.

"And I'll really get a chance to use the formula?" I tried to imagine warm winds on my bare skin.

"You bet you will."

"OK, when do we start?"

"Not so fast. Before we get into the tenure thing, there are a couple of things that need attending to."

Which is how I ended up holding the bag outside Leda Kalita's apartment while he threw down his shaving things, her love letters, some jewelry he thought might be worth money, and how it happened to be me that went to the pawn shop to see what I could get for the stuff; you can't hock things when you're invisible.

When I came back Ivor said, "Well, obviously that isn't enough money."

"You said you were going to get those letters out of my dossier."

"You bet. But first we have to do a couple more things."

So at the bank it was me that created the diversion by trying to take out all the academic vice-president's personal savings, while Ivor slipped behind the counter as neatly as you please and began schlepping bags of money toward the door. Why nobody saw them floating I do not know, because by that time I was engaged in a fullscale tantrum on the floor of the bank so that guards came, tellers came, a doctor came, by that time I was pretty sure Ivor had gotten away with the money and so just as they were about to sock me full of Thorazine I sat up and told them it was a scene I was working up for acting class. Hell yes it was embarrassing, but it worked, and Ivor promised to remove the bank's letter from my dossier just as soon as I helped him do a couple more things.

With the money he bought out the laboratory of crazed old Dr. Knox, who was fired from our college years ago because he believed it was possible to program plants to differentiate between people and, having done so, to teach them to kill. Don't ask me what Ivor wanted with the stuff, all I can tell you is that he moved it all into the basement of my split level and after he'd set it up he wouldn't let me come in. I could hear him rattling around down there until all hours.

I left him to it because by that time I was consoling Leda Kalita, who had called me just as she found the things missing, all Ivor's belongings plus her favorite ruby ring. She wanted to cry on my shoulder, under the circumstances there was nothing I could tell her that would help and so I just held her and patted her on the back, I'll admit, it felt really good.

She said, "I don't know what to think. One minute he was with me and the next, ffft, without a trace."

"That's terrible." I held her but I kept one eye open. "And the jewelry."

"I don't know what happened to him, whether he's all right or whether he's lying dead somewhere . . . Oh Sam, he was getting very strange there toward the end."

"I bet he was."

"And not getting tenure seemed to push him off. He was furious, he was making all kinds of threats, and then . . ." She was too broken up to go on.

"Ffft," I said, to help her out.

"That's it. Ffft."

"Forget him, honey, he wasn't worth it anyway."

The next thing I knew Ivor had bought out a florist's shop, or maybe it was a greenhouse. There were bushes in the stairwell, begonias in the living room and bromeliads in the kitchen, and I didn't like the way they were looking at me. I tried to ask him about it but he was getting testier and testier, and when I accused him of being short with me he said if I didn't like it I could forget about getting tenure, worse yet, I would never work again.

I let Leda comfort me. I couldn't tell her my troubles so I would let her tell me hers, how Ivor was insanely preoccupied during his last days, how right before he left he promised to come back for her.

I said, "I wouldn't count on that."

Her eyelashes were spiky with tears. "You wouldn't?"

"A lot of men are rats." I put my arms around her.

I thought I heard a snicker. *Bastard,* I thought, *at a time like this,* but there was nothing I could do or say to get him out of the room.

So I think Ivor was sitting on the desk in her crowded office while Leda and I played our first love scene: the hugging and mutual confession, yes I felt lonely in a crowd, I too often wondered where it was all leading, I was afraid of not getting tenure but she should not be, we scientists all know the arts are easy sledding; I think Ivor was there throughout our mutual discovery, the murmuring and increasing warmth . . .

"Oh Sam," she said, "something just brushed my hair."

"Imagination." I thought I heard a door slam. "Now, about you and me . . ."

So it was me and Leda after that, Leda and me. That night at dinner when Ivor came down in my best bathrobe, I said, "Ivor, why did you have to treat poor Leda that way?" He was wrapped tightly in the bathrobe but he had gotten careless about the ski mask, so I looked him right in what I thought might be the eye.

"Never mind," he said, a little huffily, I thought. "Part of the master plan."

"About this master plan. You never told me there was going to be a master plan. You just said you wanted me to do a couple of little things and you would do a few little things for me."

"By the way," he said as if I hadn't even spoken. "I got rid of those unfavorable letters today, you know, the ones in your promotion folder? And I put in some substitutes I wrote myself, pretty good forgeries if I do say so. I made you out to be the next Nobel candidate."

"I'm very grateful, Ivor. Then our relationship is more or less at an end?" I could hardly wait to get rid of him and his plant collection. I couldn't stand the way he sat around totally expressionless, it gave me the creeps, the way he kept sneaking up on me.

He put down his fork. "Well, if you want it that way. Of course you haven't had your turn at the formula, you know, naked power?"

I was thinking about Leda. "That doesn't seem so important now."

"That's all very well," he said, "but of course there is the matter of Dean Plotkin's opposition to your case."

"What—about—Dean—Plotkin's—opposition?"

"Well, frankly, those letters I put in your file almost did the trick, you were almost home free, but you might as well know I was almost home free too, I was just about to get tenure when, well, it's this last little thing that's the pitfall. Dean Plotkin can ruin every thing."

"What are you talking about?"

"Plotkin. He's old, but he's powerful, he can turn the whole department against you in a flash."

"All right, Ivor, what do you want me to do?"

Which is how I ended up distracting the guards at the Lifman Institute while potted rubber plants floated by behind them, and how I ended up in the bushes outside Dean Plotkin's dining room window letting Ivor stand on my shoulders so he could put a geranium inside.

"But I don't see what this is going to do?"

"Just wait," Ivor said. "My plants will do it for us."

"Do what?"

He only said, "You'll see."

All right, I didn't know how deep I was in. I didn't know what the plants were going to do, and by the time I found out things were happening so fast that there was no way for me to extricate myself. Unwittingly, I had helped Ivor inaugurate his master plan. The first thing was, when I got to the office the next morning everybody was talking about Dean Plotkin. He was out sick, mystery disease, terrible symptoms, nobody knew what was the prognosis. I was pondering that when I picked up the afternoon papers and read about the mystery epidemic sweeping the Lifman Institute.

"Ivor, what does this mean?"

"You wanted Plotkin out of the way, didn't you?"

I shook the paper at him. "But *this.*"

"It was Lifman's letter that kept me from getting tenure. He knew about my invisibility research, he thought he could get rid of me and then . . ." He read the paper, laughing. "Don't you see? Revenge."

"But Ivor, everybody in the whole building is sick."

"That'll teach Lifman to fool around with me."

"But what if they die?"

"Shut up and let me enjoy this," Ivor said.

I was frightened, riddled with guilt, wondering what to do about Ivor and how you could turn in somebody who was invisible, but each day something happened to keep me from acting. The department met on me without Dean Plotkin and voted to forward my promotion to the advisory committee. If the committee liked me, I was as good as promoted, and I couldn't do anything to jeopardize that. Furthermore, Leda seemed to like me better and better, she invited me over at odd hours, and made all kinds of promises. So I was torn, I was happy about the promotion, about Leda, but at the same time there were shadows: all those people sick, Ivor clanking in the cellar, the demands he made on me.

When he robbed a place to fund his projects, it was me holding the bag outside while he floated the money through the window. Some of the work embarrassed me, I especially hated creating diversions in department stores, or at the bank, but by that time I had gone too far to turn back.

Ivor was working on the Advisory Committee for me, reporting all their secret deliberations, and I was so close to my goals that I couldn't afford to let him stop. At the same time his activity in our cellar was getting more and more frenetic; bigger and more dangerous plants moved in every day and Ivor sent me out for more expensive and more suspicious ingredients to use in his deadly formula. I couldn't stop him and I couldn't get him to tell me what he was doing. I couldn't even refuse to help him or he would go to the promotion committee and put terrible letters about me in their files.

Around that time Leda became strangely distracted. She was always glad to see me when she was home, but she was hardly ever home. By that time we were sort of semi-engaged, but when I tried to find out where she went at night she would only shut me off. Ivor had made me help him move plants into the house of an old enemy, and the whole family was sick. What's more we knocked over a jewelry store and he tripped the alarm so we almost got caught. That night in bed I couldn't sleep for trembling. The more I thought about it the worse I felt because it was obvious who would be arrested if we did get caught. Ivor would drift away in the night and it was me they would drag off to prison, me, the visible partner. It was my house that was filled with the incriminating evidence, it was me that would go to jail while Ivor drifted back to eat my food and use all the conveniences until he had exhausted my resources; then he would just drift off and find some other sucker to play. The more I thought about it the worse I felt. I wasn't any closer to being promoted than I had been when we first made our agreement. My life was no better because of my association with Ivor; if anything, it was worse.

"Things aren't any better, Ivor."

"These things are slow." I think he was sitting on the corner of my coffee table.

"Ivor, it's been three months."

"Shut up or I'll sic the plants on you."

"That's another thing."

"I'm warning you."

"Don't try it." I raised my secret weapon: a can of spray paint. I spritzed the corner of the coffee table, to show him I meant business. "This stuff is indelible."

"All right, all right," Ivor said. "How would you like your turn with the formula?"

"I don't know, Ivor." I kept the can at the ready. "What's in it for me?"

"Would I con you? You can go to the ballet, mess around in the girls' dressing room."

"It's too late for that."

"All right," Ivor said. "They're meeting on your case for the last time today. Frankly, you're still in trouble. You can be there at the finish, rearrange their minds. A whisper here, a diversion created there. You know it's a paper vote, and at the last minute you can just switch papers."

"And they won't know?"

"Sam, you'll be invisible."

I was mulling it. I had more than one reason to want that. I thought Leda might be cheating on me. I put down the spray can. "All right. No tricks?"

"Would I con you?"

He made quite a ceremony of it, bringing me a little vial of the formula and making me stand in front of a mirror while I drank it so we could both watch. I said, "How do I know this isn't poison?"

"Don't be a schmuck."

First I thought the top of my head was coming off. I dropped the vial and staggered around trying to keep my skull from exploding. When that was over I felt a sensation of enormous lightness, coupled with vertigo, and when I could see again I was terrified because the only things showing in the mirror were a shirt and tie. "Ivor."

"You see?"

I stripped off the clothes, realizing as I did so that there was no reason to be embarrassed because I couldn't see Ivor and he couldn't see me. I was alone and free. "Ivor. It's wonderful."

He was capering and crowing. "What did I tell you? Sam? Sam?"

Son of a bitch, he couldn't find me. I laughed like a lark and took off.

It was wonderful. I stole food for lunch and ate standing up stark naked in the faculty dining room. I crashed a couple of board meetings and when it was time I went to the room where the Advisory Committee meets. When the secretary went in to put folders at each place along with the pencils and clean scratch pads, I just followed her in.

Ivor. That bastard lied. The first thing I noted was that all the rotten letters were still in my dossier, plus one or two. Ivor had not done a damn thing for me. I thought I would take them and escape while I still could but by that time the committee was filing in. That was the second thing. Dean Plotkin was alive and well, and he was going to testify. It hadn't been Ivor's plant that put him in the hospital, it was appendix, and now he was just fine. Another thing: he wanted to speak in my favor, so that was the third lie. By that time I was thinking: Ivor, you bastard, what are you trying to do to me?

The provost was saying, ". . . the matter of these letters, they look very bad to me."

There was Dean Plotkin, that I had tried to remove: "But he's a brilliant teacher, and I think you need to make allowances."

"That's all very well," the provost said, "but there is the matter of this extra document. It just came today."

My colleagues all looked astounded. "What document?"

By that time I was hanging over the provost's shoulder, unbeknownst to everyone, and there it was, all done up in triplicate, I was able to get close enough to recognize the tracks of my own typewriter and Ivor's handwriting in the margins, I only caught a couple of the phrases but I knew I was in trouble so I did a stupid thing. I made a grab for it.

"What the . . ."

The provost was too quick for me and so I had to push over his chair and climb on his chest before he could recover and try to take the thing away from him. We were grappling when I became aware of voices rising behind us: the committee and my respected senior colleagues, all staggered, astounded, in full cry.

"Great Scott."

"Why this is . . ."

"What is it?"

"It's a, it looks like . . ."

"It's taking shape. It's the candidate."

"He's naked!"

"Disgraceful."

"Disgusting."

"Get off the provost, you bandit."

"Idiot, what are you doing without any clothes?"

I fell back then and got off the provost to find them all staring at me with expressions ranging from shock to revulsion. Poor old Dean Plotkin was shaking his head and saying:

"Oh Sam, I had such high hopes for you."

"What can I say?"

"You realize this is the end of your career."

I was backing away fast. "I guess it wore off. I certainly never intended . . ."

"I think you'd better get out, you may stay out your contract at this institution but I will ask you never to appear on this campus again. Your checks will be mailed to your home." Our president made a lunge for me. "You . . . You."

Dean Plotkin stepped between us. "Oh Sam, what possessed you?"

"You want to know what possessed me?" I made a grab for the president's topcoat and used it to cover my nakedness. "I'll tell you what possessed me." I was getting madder. "Somebody sold me a bill of goods."

By that time I knew exactly what I was going to do. I pulled the president's topcoat around me and headed for Leda's office. She would get me some clothes and once I had them, I was going to effect my revenge.

When I got there her door was partly open. There was somebody with her; I recognized the voice.

"But Ivor, he never hurt you."

"They were going to give him tenure instead of me. It was his fault, all of it."

"But this kind of revenge. Haven't you gone too far?"

He ignored her. "Naturally I want to thank you for keeping him occupied. And now, on to phase two."

I peeked around the door. You can imagine how eerie it looked. The bitch was sitting on his lap. "Phase two?"

"The destruction of the university," he said, "and then—"

"And then?"

"With my plants I can terrorize the world."

"Not those little house plants. . . ." She meant the ones in my basement. When had she been in my basement? Had she been there with him? I was rigid with rage.

"No. The big ones, at the Ajax warehouse. I'm going to insinuate them into high places, and then . . ."

"The Ajax warehouse?"

"Nobody knows about that but you and me. Leda, together we can do anything."

"Oh darling," Leda said. Her half of the embrace grew more intense.

I left them there.

I will not attempt to describe my emotions. I will only tell you what I did. First I went home and dressed, in black so I would be hard to see. Then I got a can of gasoline and set fire to the house. There is, after all, nothing left for me here. When Ivor goes back he will find a gaping pit because the fire exploded a gas main and everything went, house, formula, poison plants and all. If he needs the formula to stay invisible, then he will be up the creek. If he needs the formula to regain visibility, then he is in trouble too. With no place to go he will come to the Ajax warehouse, that he thought was his secret alone, and when he does he will discover that I have cut off the electricity. In the dark we will be equal, Ivor and me. He will come directly to the fuse box and because it is so dark he will not see me crouching with my spraygun, he will know nothing of my presence until I let him have it with the luminous paint.

I will let him have it with the paint and then I will be shut of him. I will send him streaking through the night like a Roman candle, knocking over plants, roaring into the streets. Maybe the paint will kill him but I hope it doesn't kill him right away. Maybe it will only burn him badly, maybe if the invisible outer layer burns off he will run away from me like the Visible Man the children put together out of plastic parts, with fatty layers, muscle, ganglia all raw and visible, everything showing but the skin.

Frontiers

Every time he left home Gunnar Morgan had the same misgivings: as he kissed Anne and the twins goodbye he was visited by all the farewell scenes in all those old Westerns: the settler kissing the wife and young ones and going off to town only to come back and find the homestead flattened, with an Indian spear planted in the wreckage and some child's rag-doll abandoned next to a naked, charred rib-cage, still smoking in the ruins. The settler would weep over the remains in the full knowledge that in such circumstances, the dead were always better off than the ones that were captured. In the mov-ies the settler always seemed surprised, while Gunnar and the rest of the audience knew ahead of time, from the moment at which they parted. Now that he had a family of his own Gunnar thought per-haps the settler had known too, but in the frontier society there were times when a man had to go ahead and do that which needed doing.

Still he held Anne too tight at the last moment; she must have guessed at some of it because she ran her hands behind her back and took his hands firmly, helping him to release her. "Gunnar, don't worry."

"Alone out here. One woman alone, with nobody but a couple of children."

"The sooner you go, the sooner you'll be back."

Why did that sound so familiar? Troubled by echoes, he said, "It's so wild out here, I just hate to leave you."

"I don't care. I like it."

He looked at the glint in her eyes and thought perhaps she did. "Take care of yourself."

She lifted her head. "I always do." She seemed compelled to add: "The girls like it too."

"Oh Anne, please be careful."

"Don't worry, there's nothing out here."

"Still . . ." What was he afraid of, really?

"Gunnar, go!" She was about to lose her temper. It was hard, he supposed, all of them shut in here with no place to go and no place to be alone. These days he and Anne grappled over the smallest issues, sawing back and forth over each petty decision. At the end she always smiled and deferred to him, saying, "After all, you're the boss here." In another circumstance she would be boss and they both knew it; he blamed himself for these clashes; it was his fault that they were stuck out here; he put her lapses down to cabin fever.

The twins were hanging on his waist. "Bring us a present from Flagstaff, Daddy."

Reluctant to let go of Anne's fingers, he looked down at them: Jenna, who moved like a willow whip, and practical little Betsy. "What do you want me to bring you?"

Betsy said, "A book I haven't read."

Jenna's face blossomed. "Anything, just as long as it's pretty."

"I never should have brought you to this Godforsaken place," he said over their heads. "You should have friends, you should be going to exciting places."

Anne lifted her head with an odd smile. "This will have to do for the time being." She was helping him to leave. "I need you to go now, we're running out of everything. And if you can find that fabric I've been waiting for, it will make all the difference."

"Oh Anne." His voice failed him.

"Hurry. When you get back, we'll have a party."

"I love you, Anne."

"I know it."

She'll be all right, he told himself, riding out. This is a different story altogether. He waited outside the dome until she had secured the airlock. Now nothing could get in or out and as far as he knew, nothing moved in the vast, dead lands outside it. Anne had sidearms and emergency beepers in addition to the laser cannon, but his heart contracted every time he had to go away and he would walk with his jaw taut and his shoulders high until he came riding back over the last ridge and saw her standing next to the airlock, waving to him through the dome's tough, transparent surface.

He had to go to Flagstaff to pick up supplies and a new chip for his communicator because the thing kept missing digits, which meant he also had to deliver the month's observations to the government office in person. Before the cataclysm everything was easier; computer systems were reliable and they could be checked and augmented by voice transmission. After the failure of Fail-Safe and the cataclysm, a great many things simply stopped working. Even now, with civilization more or less reassembled, they were still not working. Gunnar felt badly about this but, he thought, he owed his job to the disaster. How would he keep Anne and the twins without it? They lived in comfort in the dome, maintaining one of the outposts Gunnar had established. It was Gunnar's job to collect data because somebody in Washington reasoned that if the air ever cleared, it would happen first in the remote areas. How long would it take? Would it ever happen? Gunnar did not know; he only knew that he had to go on as if this would happen because, when there is no choice, hoping is always better than not hoping.

Flagstaff depressed him. It was crowded and ugly under the enormous dome, with too many people clogging the passages, all looking gaunt and frantic.

It always took him a week to finish his business, not because he had that much to do but because of the lines at the government offices. He shaved the time a little by sleeping in the waiting room instead of paying someone to hold his place at night, but he tossed restlessly, and when he did sleep he dreamed of painted savages swarming over the ramparts in enormous numbers. At the supply depot, he could not find half the things Anne had asked for. There was flawed fabrics, meat tinned in spite of the maggots, weevily flour. He did the best he could, knowing whatever he brought, Anne would pretend to be delighted. Then she would take it and transform it as she had the outpost, making pretty little curtains and tablecloths, constructing beautiful dinners out of the meanest ingredients.

Oh Anne. He had robbed her of her job and her society; they both pretended she could sell her designs from the outpost and if she could not—well, he was going to figure out some way for her to get them to the fashion center. Until he did, it was important for him to encourage her to keep working and for both of them to pretend this was somehow possible. He bought her a piece of artificial turquoise and picked up some candy for the twins and, as an afterthought, a bit of colored glass for Jenna. Then he headed out across the darkening badlands, already imagining what Anne would have prepared for the homecoming dinner, what he would say when the twins swamped him with the drawings they had made to surprise him. In the ruined world he fixed on the life at home, which he had wrought with his bare hands and which would be going on as always, waiting for him to walk back into it. Once he had shut himself in and sealed the airlock, he could believe the world was at rights because, inside the dome, he and Anne tried to make the life they wanted.

Leaving Flagstaff, he thought the color of the sky had altered in the week he had been there. He was certain the air was denser. Sunset bloodied the desert and as the broken shells of buildings outside the dome gave way to broken rock shapes and ruined mesas, shadows fell like knifeblades across the path Gunnar traveled. Once he thought he saw something moving and he kicked the air-cushion on the scooter a little higher and checked the shield. He told himself this was routine; after all, these were contaminated lands and he needed to protect himself, but he was running the scooter too fast and he understood that there was more. He had the idea that something had changed, there were strange forces stirring. What was the matter? Just nerves, he told himself: too many days away from the family, but that did not explain it. He could not say exactly what he feared, only that he feared it. He would not feel easy until he had ridden up over the last rise and could see Anne under the lights inside the airlock, waving. It was near dawn by the time he made the approach and as the sky began to pale he started in alarm and jerked around to look at the long ridge off to his right. In the flash before he turned and saw nothing he had imagined he saw this: a frieze of people naked as the figures on a Greek urn, streaming over the crest and away from him.

Coming downhill, he was relieved to see the dome exactly as he had left it. There were Anne's plants in hanging baskets, just inside the airlock; the emission tube was steaming, which meant that she was preparing his homecoming dinner in spite of the hour. He strained to see her and when he did not he thought she must be in the house, releasing the catch for the decontamination hangar. He gunned the scooter inside, started the process and waited until the gauges told him it was safe.

Everything was as he had left it. Anne's little garden was flourishing under the artificial light; she had picked tomatoes for the homecoming meal and left them in the grass. He was surprised to see the knife stuck into the earth next to them; usually she was not so careless. He picked up the basket and went to the house, calling.

"Anne, I'm home."

When she did not answer he thought she must be in the bathroom; the rotten supplies made them sick more often than they would have admitted.

"Anne," he said a little louder. "Are you all right?"

He imagined he heard her answer.

"I brought in the tomatoes."

The sound turned out to be the kettle whistling in the neat little kitchen. The sauce was just beginning to burn off the cutlets she had been making. He turned off the stove and went down the hall.

"Anne, are you in there?"

The bathroom turned out to be empty.

"All right, if you're hiding, I give up."

Nobody answered and nobody came.

"Game's over, OK?"

He went into the twins' room. Jenna's bed had not been slept in. She was like a little spook sometimes, flitting around the dome in the middle of the night; they would find her asleep in the garden the next morning. Betsy had been in her bed not five minutes ago; there was the dent her head left in the pillow. He put his face in it, smelling the young girl smell of soap and musk and candy. It was still warm.

"Come on, dammit, everybody."

He was tired, it did not seem like a good game; they weren't in the house and he searched the garden in growing exasperation. They would have to lie flat in the synthetic earth to elude him and yet he could not see anybody. He searched the house from the gable to the crawlspace underneath. In a panic, he made certain Anne's clothes were where she had left them. If she ran away where would she go anyway, and how would she get out? There was not another scooter between here and Flagstaff. Mourning, he went into the kitchen. In addition to the cutlets, Anne had been making a dessert and a bowl of cream substitute; the cream mixture was still frothing. She must have run out in a hurry. Run out. She couldn't. Their suits were still hanging by the airlock and they were good only for short distances. He would have found their bodies within a few feet of the dome.

"Oh, Anne! Is it something I did?"

His voice tore through the silence in the dome but all he heard was the reverberation, circling and coming back to mock him.

He had not really expected an answer.

Frantic, he inserted the new chip and punched an emergency message into the console. FAMILY MISSING. UNEXPLAINED. All he got back was the usual: MESSAGE BEING PROCESSED. It would be days before they got back to him. He got in the scooter and began sweeping the surrounding wastelands in widening circles, not because he thought he would find them alive, even if he did find them, but because a portion of his life had been stolen and he would not feel right until he could restore it. Circling hopelessly, he called them by name, not because he imagined they would hear him through the shield or across the terrifying distances, but because he could imagine they were still his at least for as long as he kept calling them. By the time he gave up altogether, which was not for several weeks, he had covered hundreds of miles, ranging wide in spite of his fears, the sinister shadows and crevices in the empty, blasted lands.

Finally the terminal acknowledged his first transmission:

ABSENCE UNEXPLAINED.

He sent back: PLEASE EXPLAIN IT.

DON'T WORRY.

EXPLAIN. He tapped out this last in growing impatience. The exchange had taken several weeks and when he returned from his last foray the terminal was displaying what would turn out to be the last message on the subject.

THIS KIND OF THING HAPPENS ALL THE TIME.

"Like hell it does!"

It was almost more than he could bear, he thought, and he tapped in his last response: BUT THEY LOVED ME.

Preparing for yet another sweep he stopped, suddenly, in the middle of filling his pack with provisions. He was riveted by Anne's cutlets, petrifying in their sauce. The mold growing on the abandoned cream substitute filled him with sadness, and then anger. *Damned if I'll eat her food,* he thought, *not until I've had an explanation.*

Whose fault was this, anyway, his, for leaving them alone, or hers, for being careless? What were the last things they'd said to each other? He scoured his memory, trying to remember her exact tone the last time he saw her. What was it? Love, or exasperation? If the latter, whose fault was it, his, for bringing her out here to this awful place, or hers, for losing faith? Should he have loved her better or was it her fault, for not loving him, or was it out of their hands altogether?

It came to him in a flash. *This is not my fault. It is beyond my power.*

He would settle in here, and try to reconcile himself. In the next second, of course, his mouth went dry and his heart thudded to a stop: *My God, what if somebody out there stole her?*

KIDNAPPERS? He tapped it into the console.

IMPOSSIBLE. It took a week for this response to come: a week in which he reluctantly disposed of the last meal Anne had cooked for him, and began setting the house to rights. The letters formed: ENVIRONS UNINHABITABLE.

UNINHABITABLE REALLY?

The machine corrected itself. UNINHABITED.

"Then this is all her fault. Hers," he said aloud, although at the moment he could not have said whether or how this followed.

Now that he had the house shipshape, he gave up looking for them, on the premise that the next move was not his, but hers. Once he had begun keeping up the place and performing his duties in a regular way, he found himself immeasurably comforted by routine and gave himself to the solace of ritual. He did not know what he was going to do without his wife and children but at the same time he found he had plenty to do: there were the observations to record and transmit; he had to keep the place tidy; he needed to plan and make and clean up after meals, he had to exercise. He occupied almost all of their kingsized bed now, sleeping spreadeagled, and he told himself again and again that this was wonderful: the peace and quiet.

Then why did he find himself standing under the dome in the middle of the night, waking from a sound sleep to find himself drenched with sweat and screaming at the red-rimmed moon:

"You bitch, how could you do this to me?"

When it was time to make another run to Flagstaff, he secured the dome as best he could and got in the scooter with a premonitory chill: as if at strange footsteps approaching. He shook it off and kicked the scooter into high, running quickly into the city. When he got back this time with his scooter laden with supplies, he thought at first that nothing had been disturbed. Everything in the dome seemed right but not quite right; it took him several hours to locate the difference. All the presents he had brought in after the last trip, and abandoned in a corner of the twins' room, were missing.

He woke before dawn with a roaring in his ears and his insides trembling. He ran out and battered like a moth against the inside of the dome, plastering himself against the transparent surface. In the next fevered seconds he either did or did not see a wild procession peeling off from a circle in the desert; he could not be certain because they were already at the top of the ridge, pouring over the horizon; even if he did see this he could not know whether it was illusion or whether that was really Anne with hair flying and naked breasts gleaming in the poisoned air, running along with them. He threw himself onto the scooter and hurtled out, cursing the seconds it took to move through the ejection stages. Delayed as he was, he knew if there was anything out there he would catch up with it in a matter of seconds. By the time he came over the ridge, there was no moving and no trace of anything.

"Oh Anne," he shouted to the deadlands.

Then he thought: *It's your fault I'm going crazy.*

What would he do if he did come upon her, cowering in the rubble? He did not know.

He searched for a long time.

That night he slept without dreams, and when he woke he was weeping.

After that, he got hold of himself. He added several new elements to his routine: the late-morning coffee, the afternoon drink. He liked being alone, he thought. He had always liked it.

If this was true, then what was the matter with him? He found himself pressed against the dome at odd hours, staring into the night without being sure how he got there. Once he thought he saw somebody staring in: a naked man, the color of the red sand; he thought he saw other naked people standing in the shadows behind him.

Another time he imagined he saw Anne and the twins and another time, the naked man with Anne at his shoulder.

In the morning everything always looked more or less the same, and by the time Gunnar had finished his morning rounds, the fevered visions would have faded.

Still one night when a sudden wind swept away most of the haze, he saw them again and this time he was certain the savage, if that was what it was, had something bright on a thong at its throat, and touched it just before it laughed and vanished: the turquoise he had brought Anne from Flagstaff.

Damn you Anne! Damn you anyway.

He knew he could not have seen this because nothing could live out there. Still he hardened his heart against her.

Then when he least expected it, he was waked by her calling.

Gunnar, Gunnar, please.

He sat up in bed, certain he had been dreaming. He sat in the dark with his eyes wide and his jaws open as if that would help him hear better.

The dome reverberated with her pounding. *Please, Gunnar.*

"Go to hell," he said aloud, and then covered his head with pillows. She had put him through too much; she was gone forever; he could live with that. Still he could hear the drumming. He reached for the sleeping capsule he always kept next to the bed and crunched it between his teeth.

When he woke it was still night; the sky outside was touched with beginning light and Anne, if it was Anne, was still out there.

He ran outside. It was her, or somebody who looked just like her, splendidly naked, pressing herself against the dome and calling.

"Go away."

Did she answer? *Oh Gunnar, please let me in.*

"I can't, you're dead."

Not dead. Changed.

"Oh Anne, why did you leave me?"

I didn't leave you, I was taken.

The thought shook him with rage. "You don't love me."

She threw her hands in the air. *I couldn't help it.*

"Now I suppose you want to come back."

Oh Gunnar, please. I want to come home. We all do. The twins came out of the murk and stood next to her: taller, beginning to be women.

"Where were you? Where were you all this time?"

Oh Gunnar, it doesn't matter.

He was torn; caution and resentment pulled him one way, desire the other. "If you loved me, you never would have gone."

We couldn't help it. Really. Please let us in.

He said, "I can't," but his hands were already pressed against hers, separated only by the dome's glassy surface. He was thinking about the apparitions in the night: the savage with the flash of turquoise at the throat; he was thinking about what she and the savage would have done and he was both enraged and maddened. "This is impossible. Everything outside is poison."

That's what you think.

"The air is poison."

That's only what you think. She danced back a few steps and shook herself.

"You must be poison."

She threw back her head and lifted her arms. *Do I look poison?*

He cried out, putting all the loss and frustration of the last months into his voice: "What were you *doing* all this time?"

Don't make me stand out here begging. Then she added that which he needed to hear to make what came next possible. *I love you.*

He thought he knew what he was letting into the dome: doubt and anger, along with whatever contamination their bodies would have collected, but Gunnar found himself moving toward the airlock in spite of himself, passing trembling hands over the dials and switches that would open it to her, and as he did so he could feel his throat close and his body quicken with a sweet, wild desire.

He hesitated.

This might be a trick.

She might be trying to destroy him.

He realized it didn't really matter.

She was back, enhanced by her absence and whatever had happened to her in it and he knew he would have her.

"I love you too," he said and threw the last switch. The last seal opened and she came in to him, and even as he held out his arms and Anne walked into them without apology or explanation, he could see the twins tumbling in behind her, could see the crazed look in Betsy's eyes, which were all whites, the fact that Jenna's teeth were bared; in the second before he buried his face in Anne's neck he saw lodged in Jenna's dense hair: the jawbone of some long-dead small animal; two brightly colored feathers.

Dog Days

Coming home through the park that afternoon, Norton Enfield was both glad and sorry he didn't have Dirk along. As long as they kept Dirk hidden at home the dog was safe and so was everything in the apartment. As Myrna would say, the loss of his pocket money would be little enough to pay. Furthermore Enfield was never quite comfortable with the dog; Dirk moved with velvet grace, barely suffering Enfield's hand upon his leash, and he had to admit that he felt more at home facing muggers and deviates and other assorted perils than he did under the dog's unwavering yellow gaze. He had always been made uneasy by the Doberman's aura of compressed power, the glittering teeth and the steel spring muscles under the glistening hide. Dirk would watch him and Myrna, looking from one to the other as they spoke, and more than once Enfield had drawn his wife into the kitchen so that they could have a word alone because he could not fight down the growing conviction that the dog understood and disapproved of everything he said. Still with Dirk along Enfield would not have lost his wallet, no mugger would have dared attack him and they certainly would not have beaten him up; instead Enfield would have had the pleasure of watching Dirk rip their throats out before either of them could cry for help.

He had left Dirk home because Myrna insisted: the pollution squads were fanning ever wider on their search and destroy missions and there were civilian vigilantes with nets and loaded automatics lurking behind every bush. As he left the apartment it had crossed his mind that if he lost Dirk he and Myrna would be alone at last, but Myrna had said, simply, "You're not taking Dirk, not with things the way they are," and the dog had shown a sliver of teeth in the beginning of a snarl.

Dirk was Myrna's dog, really; she had brought him home after she was mugged in the elevator for the fourth time in a week. Enfield had come home from work to find her in the living room with a spindly-legged puppy which did not slobber or galumph the way puppies were supposed to, but instead lifted its head like a racehorse and looked at him out of one white-ringed eye.

"What's that?"

"My protection." Myrna was coiled on the floor next to the dog, looking up at him through a fall of dark, glossy hair. "Isn't he adorable?"

The dog's head was diamond shaped, like a serpent's head, and it gave him a mature, calculating look. Enfield said, "What's his name?"

And Myrna, who had always called Enfield Norty, and mocked him for not having a name like a dagger, said, "Dirk. He's sweet, he's a beautiful boy. Dirk Storm."

"Now I suppose you're going to put off having the baby."

"Just for a while." Silken, graceful in some of the same ways the pup was, she had tilted her head. "After all, he *is* going to have to be trained."

So the dog had been Myrna's from the beginning, and it watched Enfield's every move with calculation, straining forward on its haunches when Enfield moved to embrace his wife, growling deep in its throat when Enfield raised his voice. More than once he had waked with a start, almost certain he heard it breathing somewhere in the room, and he could not embrace his wife in bed without thinking of the dog. Even though Dirk was locked in the kitchen, Enfield could not free himself of the image of the dog poised on the dresser, ready to spring at the slightest untoward move. Even though Dirk had saved him from a mugging more than once and had savaged a burglar in the foyer and so perhaps saved his life, Enfield had always regarded Dirk with mixed emotions. So it was with mixed emotions that he had watched the civilian vigilantes go into action, and he could not share Myrna's chagrin when the mayor chose his Sunday night music show to announce the creation of what he euphemistically called the antipollution squad.

"It's *murder.*" Myrna couldn't stop crying. "It's like the concentration camps."

"The dogs are sticking to the sidewalks, Myrna. We're knee-deep in droppings and they're tearing little kids to pieces in the streets."

"Their mothers ought to take better care of them."

"I'm afraid it's gotten beyond that," Enfield had said. "It's gotten out of hand."

So it was that as he came home through the park this particular evening he could hear the sound of distant shots and yelps of pain, snarling and outraged outcries and, nearby, a howl which rose amid the other sounds, twining around the others in incalculable woe. As he rounded the last bend, Enfield came upon the source: an old lady with her nose raised and her throat swelled in anguish over the corpse of a pet Pekingese.

"He never barked," she said when he tried to calm her, "and he never bit anybody and he hardly ever pooped, at least not so a person would notice, and I was ever so careful about him, I picked it all up with my little silver trowel and I would take it home and flush it down the toilet and oh oh oh," she said and lapsed into an open-throated, inarticulate howl.

"I'm sure he meant a great deal to you, Madam," Enfield said because he would do anything he could to get her to stop howling. "Perhaps you could have him stuffed."

"Stuffed," she cried, "stuffed," and Enfield backed away quickly; she had turned on him, in another minute she was going to tear him apart.

On the avenue another distraught dog owner fought for his life; the pollution squad had gotten his animal, and a wild dog pack had fallen upon the corpse. Now they were finished and they had turned on him, still lusting for blood. Enfield looked around for a stick or a rock, anything to help him, but there was nothing. "Save yourself," the man cried, disappearing into a maelstrom of fangs and claws. Enfield cast a quick look around for the pollution squad, thinking they might be able to do something, but they must have piled into that yellow van and disappeared the minute they had done their job. After all, it was safer to go after dogs on leashes than it was to risk wind and limb going after the wild packs which hid out in the park. It was easier to follow the letter of the law and fall upon the attack-trained toy poodle, or the fat cocker spaniel following meekly on a leash. Most dog owners kept their pets inside now, or walked them under cover of night, hoping to elude the squads, which patrolled round the clock. When the squad swooped down and did its duty the owner would stare uncomprehendingly at the empty collar, the slack leash, saying, "But he begged and begged, I just had to bring him out." Those with strength of character had already freed their dogs, hoping they would be able to survive in the park. They might sneak down for an occasional midnight rendezvous; with luck they might get in a few words with the beloved pet before they had to break and run, fleeing the wild packs. Enfield wondered if Dirk would care enough to rendezvous with him or Myrna, but he knew better; at times it seemed to him that they lived to serve the dog, rather than the dog serving them.

From behind him he heard snarling and sounds which were even more sinister. It's dog-eat-dog in this day and time and that's the truth, he thought, and launched himself on the avenue.

He found it hard going; traffic had stopped moving some weeks before, which meant he had to vault rusting Volkswagens and climb over taxi bumpers to get to the other side. Abandoned automobiles took up so much room that the dogs were confined to the sidewalks, and by this time they were thick with ordure, studded with an occasional carcass and whorled with traces of scenes of gallantry or carnage, depending. Since the mayor's announcement, Sanitation had been put on the extermination detail, and there seemed to be no keeping up with the problem after that. The program was in its fifth week now and the damnable thing was that conditions seemed to be not better but worse. The strays had mushroomed in number and in addition to everything else a number of humans had taken to using the sidewalks and the parks as toilets as part of a radical movement designed to prove some kind of point.

Perhaps driven by their lack of success, the pollution squads were becoming more and more thorough and ruthless; they had begun lurking at the doorways to buildings, bribing the doormen to tip them off as to how many dogs lived there and when their owners were liable to bring them outside. At Myrna's insistence, Enfield had kept Dirk inside from the beginning. She seemed to have the idea that out of sight also meant out of mind and she had done her best to exercise the dog inside the apartment, teaching it to jump over the coffee table, ricochet against the front door and then spring into another leap. She bridled defensively when Enfield looked at the dog with even an indication of doubt, and she was determined to teach the dog to use the toilet. Enfield supposed they would weather this crisis as they had so many others, but he did not like the look the dog had developed, as if it was fully aware of the menace outside, or its fine-tuned nervousness, or the restless way it paced now that it had been denied the park. The dog, Enfield had decided, was just about to explode, and he had also decided on his way home this afternoon that he would seek the tactful moment and then slip a little poison in its dish; he had the stuff in his pocket now. Myrna need never know, and despite their subsequent vulnerability to muggers and marauders he was convinced they would be better off.

Myrna met him at the door. "Did you hear?"

"Hear what?"

"They aren't picking up enough dogs in the street. They're starting to go door to door."

Enfield looked past her at Dirk; the dog was sitting in his favorite chair, regarding him with a look so savage that he said, "Well, we're going to have to . . ."

She put her hands on his lips. "Shhh, he understands."

He gave the dog a sharp look; Dirk licked his chops. Enfield began spelling:

"W-E-'R-E G-O-I-N-G T-O H-A-V-E T-O L-E-T T-H-E-M T-A-K-E H-I-M."

She gave him a desperate, walleyed look. "He'd never let us . . ."

The dog jerked its head around.

Enfield said, "Shh."

"We'll never let them have him," Myrna said, too loud. "Did you hear that, Dirk? We'll never let them have you . . ." Her voice dropped to a whisper. "They're in the building now."

"Then they're going to get here sooner or later," Enfield said; he had the uncanny feeling that the dog knew about the poison in his pocket, "and if they do, W-E-'R-E G-O-I-N-G T-O . . ."

"No," she said, shaking her head, "I've been working on something."

The dog leapt from the chair and came to stand beside her.

The three of them jumped at the sound of thunderous knocking.

"It's them," Enfield said, and then, "what's that?"

Myrna had produced a furry object. "It's your costume."

"You're kidding."

The knocking at the door had turned to splintering kicks; in another minute they would break it down.

Myrna looked from him to the dog, which snarled. "No, I'm not kidding, Norty, it's either you or him."

"But I'm your husband." Enfield saw with alarm that there was a robe of his laid out on the couch, along with an ascot and a towel to shroud the head. "Honey, can't you . . ."

The dog crouched to spring.

"I'm sorry, he won't let me." The door was giving way. She proffered the dog suit, loving but inexorable. "I think you'd better put this on."

A Unique Service

It first occurred to him that the thing would be useful for dodging social engagements. As a prizewinning man of letters, he was much in demand at dinner parties; as an unmarried prizewinning man of letters, he was the darling of hostesses all over Cambridge, who served him up to their guests along with the Boeuf Wellington, or the rack of lamb.

"Edward Jameson," they would say, "this is *Edward Jameson,*" and in the next breath would add, at more or less the same level of enthusiasm, "The salmon was flown in from Scotland this morning, isn't it divine?"

"Are you really Edward Jameson?"

Edward would nod modestly and try to change the subject. "So what else is new?"

"Oh Mr. Jameson, did you really write all those books?"

"I'm afraid so."

"All by yourself?"

"I used a typewriter."

"Well I haven't read any of them yet but now that we've met I certainly will . . . If you could just tell me what some of them are?"

What was he supposed to say?

He never knew in these cases, any more than he knew what to say to the junior high school students who wrote in, at the rate of two a week.

Dear Mr. Jameson,

I am in the eighth grade and I have to turn in my term paper Tuesday it is supposed to be ten pages long. I thought I would write it about your early period, which is what Miss Frumkin said I had to do, so I wonder if you could write telling me when that was, and what happened during it? If you would type it double space it would be a big help . . .

Nor did he know what to do about the budding authors who wrote:

Dear Mr. Jameson,

I have read every single line you wrote starting with *Vain Wheat* and since I admire you so much I have chosen you to read my four-volume epic about the history of America from prehistoric times to the present, which is told from the point of view of Plymouth Rock. I just happen to be visiting Boston next week and we can have a nice long talk about it while I am staying at your house . . .

It seemed to him that the simplest thing would be to change his name. What if he just ran away?

There was also the problem of Alexander Hibbard, of the history department where he was serving time this year, to say nothing of the matter of Myra Krutch. Alexander quite simply hated him, but would never come out and say it and get it over with. He insisted on sniping, lounging in the doorway while Jameson gave his lectures and not even waiting for the applause to die before he pounced.

"They couldn't possibly have done that in the '90s, and I can prove it here." He would begin reading to the group at large from a series of heavily marked texts.

"That's very interesting, Mr. Hibbard," Edward would say when he could get in a word, "and I want to thank you for your views . . ."

Hibbard would follow him out of the lecture hall and across town if necessary, still quoting at him. "I don't see how anybody who claims to know as much as you do could possibly make such a stupid mistake . . ."

"I know you don't, Alexander," he would say wearily, knowing Hibbard was ready to worry this to death. At his own front door he would turn with as much politeness as he could muster. "The thing about fiction, Alexander, is that it's fiction. You can make things up." He would not go on to say the obvious: if you had a life of your own, you wouldn't sit up nights setting traps.

That would be the end of Alexander Hibbard until next time but inside the door there was another threat. His landlady was always lurking somewhere inside the townhouse, and nine times out of ten she would spring out at him before he could reach his apartment, which was at the top. She'd trap him in the vestibule or on a landing with her black peasant blouse pulled down to reveal her bony shoulders and her hands curled around her latest sheaf of verse and he could never decide which was more terrible, the verse she read to him aloud and at length every time she caught him, or the seductive passage that always came next. He had tried various tricks to elude her, from sneaking to coming up the fire escape and in the kitchen window, but she always managed to spring out at the very moment when he thought he was home free. Once she had even caught him next to the garbage pails in the middle of the night. It did him no good to tell her he was engaged to a woman in London, which was true, nor did it make much of an impression when he said he was saving himself for his work.

If he had his way he would be on a plane to London tomorrow, to scoop up his light of love, who never asked him to explain his work; together they would move to someplace like Ceylon where the tax advantage would be the maraschino cherry on the sundae of his joy and he would spin out the rest of his life in a place where nobody had ever heard of him.

Dear Mr. Jameson,

Our book club has been reading your *Yankee Trilogy,* it took a while because we only had one copy for eighty-nine of us. Now we are wondering if you could come and explain it to us, we would appreciate it ever so much if you could bring us autographed copies of your latest book . . .

Why wouldn't they leave him alone?

Jameson you bastard,

Six weeks and not one word from you about my *Pageant for Americans* that I sent you to read. I suppose you have stolen all my ideas and are going to palm them off as your own, well don't try anything or I will sue your brains out, understand?

He needed a secretary.

. . . I know you were only in Milwaukee the one night for getting the medal but my daughter says you are the father, and she ought to know . . .

He needed a lawyer.

You damn sinkhole writer you have loved my Lizzie and left her and now you have the nerve to write about her in your filthy book well you had better watch out there are ways to get even that don't cost anything and never leave a trace . . .

Maybe he needed a bodyguard.

When the phone rang these days he generally shrank from it but there was always the possibility that it was the Nobel Prize committee and so even though common sense told him this was impossible, he was always compelled to pick it up. Usually he did so against his better judgment and was sorry; this time he was not.

There was something about the caller's voice. "Fed up?"

He answered at once. "You're damn right I'm fed up."

"I think I can help you." The voice was like black velvet against naked skin on a cool night.

"How did you get my number?"

"You are Edward Jameson and your life is getting out of control."

"Is this an obscene phone call or what?"

"Too many demands and impositions," the voice of velvet said, with enormous sympathy. "I am prepared to offer you a unique service that will end this kind of thing. Our company provides a product that relieves you of unpleasant encounters and infelicitous social chores; if you're not satisfied within one day, *one day*, we guarantee your money back. Now Mr. Jameson, I'd like an opportunity to discuss this with you in person . . . if you're interested."

"I never give . . ."

". . . interviews," the velvet voice said. "Our service even takes care of that for you. Now when can we meet?"

Whoever she was, she was offering something he had to have—maybe even more—that voice! "What are you doing tonight?"

"I'll be right over."

When she came over she was not what he had thought. She was

indeed fabulously beautiful, but a beautiful sixty-five, if she was a day, with a body that was still good and silver hair and a businesslike look that told him to forget everything he had been thinking and sit still and listen to her pitch.

"How did you get my name?"

"We only approach people who need our service. Let's just say you were targeted . . ."

"Wait a minute."

"Be quiet and listen," she said.

Which he did. When she finished, all he said was, "Do you take American Express?"

"Gold card?"

"Gold card."

"Your unit will be ready by the tenth. Money back guaranteed if it's not everything we say."

He could hardly wait for delivery. It did not matter that in addition to agreeing to the handsome down payment, he had signed away a hefty percentage of his income for the rest of his life. It seemed cheap at the price. Myra Krutch had started springing out at him from every niche and alcove in the building and last night he had let himself into the apartment with a sigh of relief only to find her crouched in a corner of his own living room, staring at him with passionate eyes and reciting a new ode, which she continued to do until he took her by both shoulders and moved her out. Some jerk from North Carolina had decided Jameson had ripped off the *Yankee Trilogy* from his own unpublished memoirs and was taking him to court with lengthy quotations to prove his point. Alexander Hibbard had managed to rouse his colleagues and Jameson was facing a hearing before the massed faculties of the arts and sciences; if it went against him he was going to have to present complete documentation and produce the source books to verify every word he said in every lecture he gave for the rest of the term. His unopened mail accumulated in a shoebox, like a ticking bomb. His phone was ringing off the hook.

It was too much.

Still when the product did arrive, it was not quite the relief he had hoped. It was a relief all right, just having the unopened crate in the front hall gave him confidence, but it was disconcerting too. To begin with, when he opened the crate and looked into it, it was like running into a mirror at full speed. The product resembled him exactly. Oh there were a few differences, of course, an absence of cynical lines around the mouth, and eyes that glazed slightly, instead of crackling with intelligence, but of course he hadn't gotten the nerve to turn the thing on. He contemplated it in silence for a long time. This was the answer to all his problems and he knew it, but he was not sure what else it might be; he had a certain sense of quiet menace.

He flicked on the switch.

His simulacrum stirred. "It took you long enough."

"Don't get uppity," he said, and turned it off.

He would deal with this later, he thought, when he'd had time to go over the instruction book. Right now, he was late for work.

When he got back that night he saw a light on in his apartment: Myra Krutch, no doubt; she would have on one of those terrible négligées and she would have spent the day on another awful verse. He went up the fire escape, thinking to sneak past her and lock himself into his bedroom until she gave up.

As it turned out this was not necessary. Myra Krutch was there all right, but she was otherwise engaged, so busy in fact, that she didn't even notice him. She was reciting all right, even as she tumbled with his simulacrum on the sofa and he could not be certain, as he crept past them and reached the safety of his room, but he thought she was spouting Macaronic verse.

It did occur to him to wonder how this had happened, and he concluded finally that she had come in, thinking to surprise him, and turned the thing on. When she left, he was going to go out and turn it off.

"Oh no you don't," it said when he finally did go into the living room some hours later. "I'm irreversible once I've been warmed up."

"You mean I can't turn you off?"

"Not any more." It was regarding him from one corner of the tumbled couch; its eyes had a sated glaze. "Maybe you'd better mop up that drink we spilled."

"I beg your pardon."

"Your friend is very nice. Look, you can use that old shirt of yours to clean up with. Frankly, it's a sight."

"Wait a minute. You're here to serve me, not the other way around."

"We're going to help each other," the simulacrum said. "You stay here and write your books. I'll take care of the rest."

"It's not as easy as you might think."

"Didn't I just spare you Myra Krutch?"

"True enough." The phone was ringing. He didn't have to answer it to know it was Myra, calling to thank him for the experience. Still he proceeded cautiously. "But I want to be sure you know your place."

"Wherever you don't want to be," the simulacrum said, as if that should be obvious. "For instance tomorrow I'm going to face the faculty committee for you, I'll even look up your references if they want, and then I'm going to take the shuttle down and get a straight story for your publishers . . . which is more than you've ever been able to do."

"I suppose you're going to write my books for me too."

"Oh no," it said airily. "You can still take care of that."

"You can't give my lectures," Jameson said defensively.

"Oh can't I. I can do it better than you and I'll take care of this guy Hibbard too." The simulacrum had fixed him with an insistent stare. "All you have to do is sit home and write."

There was something about the way it said this that Jameson didn't like. He said, warily, "And what if I don't?"

It shrugged. "You've already written enough to keep a small town in snowboots for a hundred years. It's up to you."

"I see." He had to get it out of here for a while so he could think. "Listen, I'm hungry, what about you?"

"I could use a little something, as a matter of fact. Your refrigerator's like a pocketbook after taxtime."

"I'm the writer here," Jameson said. "Now listen. I'd like you to run down to Harvard Square and get us some Chicken Delight."

It hesitated, perhaps sensing a trap. "No tricks?"

"I promise. Here, I'll give you a twenty. Pick up some cole slaw and a couple of those pies. I like apple, what about you?"

Its face brightened. "Cherry would be nice."

While it was gone he rummaged through the crate and found the instruction book. It was worse than he thought. Once warmed up and running strong, the thing could not be turned off. It was guaranteed to fulfill all functions for the subject, *all functions* for the rest of the subject's life. It was stainresistant, shrinkproof and indestructible.

It did not take long for Jameson to put together the rest. He got out his copy of the contract and read it carefully. There it all was, in black and white. He gave twenty percent of his earnings to the company; *It* was perfectly capable of writing over the rest. He had taken it into his home and now it was activated. The company didn't much care what happened to him—they would have his money anyway, and every penny his books made from now on.

He supposed he ought to stay here and fight.

Just then the phone rang and he didn't have to pick it up to know it was more trouble; what's more he was sure he heard Myra Krutch on the stairway, coming back for more. If he managed to make a stand here what would he have anyway? All this aggravation, even with the hateful simulacrum to deflect some of it. What's more, he'd have to stay here and write more of those damned books.

It didn't take him five minutes to make up his mind. If the company wanted his life, they could have it, along with his fortune and his problems with the IRS. He was going to go out and . . . He didn't know what, exactly, only that he was going to go out and be somebody else.

But he had to act fast. If the thing came back too soon and caught him he would be stuck here forever, stashed in the back bedroom writing more books to make the company rich. He thought he had better not rely on speed alone; he needed a disguise.

He had a little nestegg in the sock drawer; he stuffed the money in his pockets and took off his shirt. He had spied Myra Krutch's abandoned gauze kimono peeping out from under a sofa cushion and he slipped into it and tied a scarf around his head. Then, even as he heard a key turning in his front door, he let himself out the back window and down the fire escape.

If he wanted, he could grow a beard and become a merchant seaman, or shave his head and be an actor or a prison guard; in theory at least he could do anything he wanted to—he would sneak into London and scoop up his fiancée and take off for Machu Picchu or Marrakesh. Maybe he would be a playwright or a screenwriter this time around, or a mud wrestler; if he didn't want to, he didn't have to write another word.

Right now the night sky was perforated by stars and the warm air of early April was sweet on his face. He began springing along, across the little park that bordered the house; he was running now, feeling ten pounds lighter with every step he took.

Sisohpromatem

I, Joseph Bug, awoke one morning to find that I had become an
enormous human. I lay under the washbasin in the furnished room
which heretofore had been my kingdom, an unbounded world, and
saw first that the bottom of the washbasin dripped only a few inches
above my face and that from where I lay I could see all four walls of
the room.

Then I realized that I was lying on my back. At first I thought I
would die there unless someone came and nudged me over, and then,
as I began kicking my legs, I discovered that the forelegs clung to the
edge of the washbasin and with a certain amount of manipulation I
would be able to regain my belly. Even then I hoped that once
turned, so, I would be able to crawl away and lose myself in the
woodwork which I loved.

As you must have gathered, I had not yet grasped the enormity of
my plight. So eager was I to regain my legs that I grappled with the
basin, scrambling and then losing purchase, falling back at last to
rest.

It was only then, as I lay with these new, pink legs sprawled about
me, that I understood how repulsive I had become. The new append-
ages were huge and pink, bloated like night crawlers, and they were
only four in number. My back, which pressed against the rotting
floorboards, was uncommonly tender. Gone was my crowning
beauty; gone was the brave carapace which had glittered in the dim
light, protecting me from the thousand perils which threaten a young
roach. Gone were my brilliant antennae and the excellent legs which
supported me at my waist. In place of a body which moved like
quicksilver I was left with a series of huge mounds and excrescences;
my quick form had been replaced by an untidy, ungainly, hideous
mound of flesh.

I would have despaired then, had it not been for the instinct stronger than reason, which told me that I must struggle to regain my belly, for only then would the world look right to me.

Gathering all my strength, I grappled with the washbasin again, thinking longingly of the slime which once I had gloried in, knowing that never again would I frolic in those pipes. Once again I was reminded of our revels, the races in the cracks around the bottom of the toilet, our gallant disregard for the pellets put down by the room's human occupant, the pride one felt in escaping a clumsy human foot. And because I was, after all, an insect, I drew myself together and attempted to regain my feet. Using my strange forelegs I embraced the washbasin, pulling myself up until my upper half rested upon it, inadvertently standing as I now remembered that humans did, coming abreast of a reflecting surface, and so inadvertently looking into what I would take to be my face.

I screamed for a full minute, so overcome by tremors that I fell to what I know must have been my knees, pressing my new face against the cold porcelain. Trembling, I crumpled, noticing in transit that I bent now in several directions, most notably at the waist. Instinct guided me so that I fell in a series of stages, bending and folding and coming to rest at last on my belly, and the simple fact of lying as the gods intended gave me some small cheer.

Still I might have died then, of simple horror, if a new hope had not presented itself. As I lay with my head under the washbasin I was aware of a small progress going on in the baseboard near my head.

Even though my ears had been sadly dulled I could hear them coming—bold Hugo and grumbling Arnold, with Sarah and Steve and Gloria chittering behind. They must have been drawn by my cries—surely they were coming to rescue me.

Arnold came first, looking brightly from the murk beneath the baseboard. Because I could not interpret his expression I lay silent, waiting to see what would come. Hugo pushed up beside him, studying my left elbow, and the others came out, rank on rank, looking at me and talking among themselves. They looked so familiar, all those beloved faces, so concerned that I was sure they had come to help me and so, speaking softly so as not to flatten them with my huge voice, I said:

"Hugo, Arnold. Thank heaven you have come."

But they didn't answer. Instead they bowed their heads together, antennae intertwining, and although I could not make out what they were saying I was sure they were talking about me as they would never talk in my presence if I were myself again.

Pained by this, I turned at last to Gloria, who had been close to me in the way of a cockroach with another cockroach, and because she was not chattering with the rest but instead looked at me with a certain concentrated expression, I whispered, full of longing:

"Gloria, surely *you* will. . . ."

Gloria laid an egg.

Before I could help myself, I had begun to weep. Now this itself was a new experience, and so fascinated was I by the sensation, by the interesting taste of the liquid I excreted, that I forgot for a minute about the little delegation along the baseboard.

In the next moment, they attacked. Uttering cries of hatred and revulsion, taking advantage of me in my weakened state, they marched on me, crawling along my foreleg, heading toward my vulnerable face. They may even have thought to feed upon my eyes.

I cannot explain what happened next. Perhaps it was my pain and resentment toward these, my former brethren, perhaps it was only a sign of my metamorphosis; I only know that my pale flesh began to crawl and I rose, cracking my skull on the washbasin, nevertheless striking out, flailing, trying to scrape them off.

Landing in a cluster about my knees, they regrouped, and in the pause I tried to explain, to apologize, to beg them to recognize and accept me, but in the next second they attacked again. And so, goaded, I did what one cockroach has never done to another; I lashed out, first at Gloria, sending her flying against the baseboard; I could tell she was injured, but I was too angry to care. Then I squashed Sarah with my fist.

The others fled then, leaving me alone next to the basin, and as they left a strange new feeling overtook me. I had for the first time power, and as I thought on the injuries the others had done me, this new power tasted sweet. Almost without effort I rose once more, coming quite naturally to my feet. Then, because it seemed the reasonable thing to do, I struck the faucet until water came and washed what was left of Sarah off what I now knew to be my hands.

In the next few hours I discovered my kingdom anew. The room which I had always assumed to be the world was in fact rather small, bounded on four sides by walls and filled with appurtenances which I gradually identified according to their functions. Experimenting with my joints, I applied part of myself to a chair. In time, remembering what I knew of humans, I took up some of the rags laid over the back of the chair and put them on my person, working my head and arms into a large, stretchy garment designed for that purpose, and grandly tying another garment about my waist.

Garbed so, I went about the room again and again, finding at last an object with pictures on bits of paper bound together, understanding from the pictures that I had done something wrong and then regarbing myself according to what I saw.

From time to time I would go back to the basin and if I saw so much as a sign of one of my fellows, I would poke at the crevices with my shoe.

I was occupied thus when there was a sound on the other side of the door and before I could gather myself to hide, the door opened and another human—a female—let herself into the room.

She spoke, and so complete was my transformation that I understood her: "Where's Richard?"

Because I was afraid to try my voice, I answered her with a shrug.

"You must be one of his thousand cousins."

I nodded. I was somehow comforted by her phrase; I had always taken humans to be isolated, and it made me feel somehow secure to know that their families were as big as ours.

"Well, when is he coming back?"

I shrugged again, but this time it did not satisfy her. She came closer, apparently studying me, and she said, finally, "What's your name?"

"J-Joseph." Even I was pleased with the way it came out.

"Well, Joseph, perhaps we can go out for a bite and when we get back maybe Richard will be here."

I didn't know why, but I knew I wasn't ready. "I—I can't do that."

"Oh, you want to wait for him. Well, that's your business." She looked at me through a fall of red hair and for the first time I found hair attractive. She was soft all over, and, inexplicably, that was attractive too.

"But I am—hungry." I had not had anything since morning, when I found something behind the toilet bowl.

"I'll bring you a hamburger," she said. "If Richard comes while I'm gone bring him down to Hatton's." She studied me for a moment. "You know, you're not bad looking. But why on earth do you have your shirt buttoned that way?"

I will never forget what happened next. She stepped forward and fumbled with my upper garment, yanking it this way and that, patting it into place, and when she was satisfied she stepped back and said, "Not bad. Not bad at all." In the next second she had, miraculously, touched my face and in the next second, too fast for me but not for my heart, which followed her, she was gone.

How I exulted then! I whirled around the room like a spider, rejoicing in my many joints, knowing for the first time a certain pride in all my agile parts and the soft flesh which covered them, thinking that I would have the best of both worlds. I had been the largest and finest in the insect kingdom; now I would be the handsomest in the human world: a prince among cockroaches, a king among men. I spun and danced and celebrated my new body and then, in an orgy of release, I went back to the corner by the washbasin and with one of Richard's shoes I battered all the antennae which came at me from that miserable little crack.

"You, Ralph. Hugo. Now I understand. The lesser will always hate the great."

I was talking thus when a strange weakness overcame me, so that I had to stand suddenly because my beautiful joints had betrayed me and would not bend. Instead I stayed on my feet next to the room's one window, looking out on the world below and thinking that once I had eaten my strength would return and I would go out into it, a man among men.

And I would take the female with me. Now that she had seen me she would have no more use for this shabby Richard, who lived in this tiny, wretched room. She and I would find a nest of our own, and then . . . The thought dizzied me and I backed into a soft place set on four legs and because I could no longer remain upright without a tremendous effort I settled back in the softness, lying with a certain degree of discomfort on my back.

I was lying, so, noticing a certain strangeness about my mandibles, when a male, probably Richard, opened the door and came in the room.

In the next second he saw me lying in what I assume is his bed and some new transformation must have overtaken me for the face of which I was so proud did not please him at all, nor did my shape, lying among his bedcovers, nor did the limbs which I waved, calling out for him to stop screaming and wait.

I can hear his voice downstairs now, screaming and screaming, and I hear a female bellowing the alarm and I hear the voices of many men and know that they are armed. They are on the stairs now with chains and clubs and in my fear I find that large as I am I can move again, half this, half that, and I make my way to the basin and try to fit beneath it, and I cry out, pleading with my brethren to let me join them.

"Hugo, Arnold, let me come back."

I am trying desperately to make myself small against the baseboard but part of me still protrudes from beneath the basin—I can feel the air against my exposed, hardening back. They have broken down the door now, they are upon me.

Hugo, Arnold. It's me.

The Marriage Bug

REMOVES PROBLEMS INSTANTLY,

the advertisement read.

STICK ONE UNDERNEATH YOUR BEDSIDE TABLE
BUY ONE FOR THE KITCHEN TOO

Well she did, she ordered two through the mail (five hundred dollars in advance for the first one, fifty percent off for each additional unit), what she had to do to get the money was too embarrassing to remember, and she could hardly wait until the package came.

The thing was, her marriage to Anthony was getting worse with every passing day. She didn't know what she had expected, beyond Mr. and Mrs. on the mailbox and monogrammed pillowcases and never having to go back to the Heartsease Singles Club, but she certainly deserved better than this. He hardly ever came home before midnight any more, and when he did he was so filled with the details of his triumph at the Jai Alai fronton that he barely noticed her; he would count his winnings into the galvanized mailbox he kept under the head of the bed on his side, where his hand could droop down and touch it while he slept, and then he would crawl in next to her in his underwear and roll over with his back turned and start to snore, leaving her to get up, weeping, and scrape their untouched midnight supper of Stouffer's and Sara Lee into the trash.

He never talked to her at breakfast, either, except to complain because his Pop Tarts were cold, but whose fault was that? Avis always tried her best for him, she would get up a full hour before the alarm so she could take the rollers out of her hair and comb it out and run a sponge around the surfaces in the living room to erase any rings his bottles of Ripple had left. Then she would get out the Pop Tarts and mix the Tang for him and make a brimming double mug of

Instakaf so she could have everything nice for him because she had promised to love and take care of him forever the day they were married in front of a nationwide audience on the "Get Rich Television Wedding Show." She would never forget the confetti and the orchestra and the pink champagne and the way she and Anthony kissed while the emcee Alphonse Hinkle lifted his hands above their heads to signal for applause and smiled and smiled and smiled.

Which is why this was so important. They had left the show under crossed boom microphones, it was by far the happiest moment of her life and, well, ever since then everything had gone downhill.

Maybe they just didn't have enough in common, she thought, a simple typist like herself and this hard-drinking fun-loving parts service manager for the Mini-Bike Service and Sales Center of Avondale. She could tell him about her day at the office but they were all alike, whereas Anthony led a life of infinite variety, bombing off to mini-bike rallies and yokking it up with the redheaded bookkeeper at the shop, in addition to which Anthony had this going to the Jai Alai fronton and on weekends he went off somewhere with his friends.

The thing was, Avis would put out the Tang and the Pop Tarts and he would come out of the bedroom and lock the door because of the money in the galvanized mailbox without even bothering to see whether she had gotten her shoes for the day. Then he would sit down in the breakfast nook and have his breakfast without saying anything and if she tried to talk to him he would just yawn and scratch and act as if he hadn't heard, and if she tried to ask him anything, like, how was your day, dear, or is that a motorcycle I heard bringing you home last night? he would just scratch and sigh and get up without finishing his second Pop Tart, even if it was raspberry, his favorite, and then he would belch and leave the house.

All right, maybe she was a little dull, even though she wore pretty-colored things and tried to put on a perky smile and read the papers every day so she would have at least one new thing to talk about. Maybe she wasn't as pretty as the redheaded bookkeeper or as interesting as his friends that he went to the Jai Alai fronton with every mortal night, but in the courtship phase he hadn't seemed to mind. In the courtship phase he sat down on the stool next to hers at the bar in the Heartsease Singles Club at the corner of Arbutus and

Nightingale, just sat down next to her one night and they hit it off. Then about a month later their hands met in the basket of cheese popcorn on the bar as they were watching a late-night rerun of the "Get Rich Television Wedding Show;" his big hand closed over her big one and their fate was sealed.

Avis knew married wasn't modern, but what did she care anyway? It was all she'd ever wanted, after all. The show was everything she had hoped for too: they were given a white dress for her and a pale blue suit with a pale yellow ruffled shirt for Anthony courtesy of the management and they got to tell their courtship story to the world, such as it was, although of course the writers for the show had to dress it up a little bit. Then after the first commercial break their friends and relatives all came on stage to surprise them in pastel tuxedos and pretty dresses also provided by the management and they had the wedding and after the second commercial break everybody threw rice and Anthony recited a poem he said he wrote especially for their wedding day that still gave her chills every time she thought of it:

> When the earth's last picture is painted
> And the tubes are twisted and dried
> Comes a pause in the day's occupation
> That's known as the turn of the tide.

She could still see his face; his eyes got all glistery when he read it, the orchestra played "Let Me Call You Sweetheart" in the minor with a beguine underneath, the studio audience applauded and she cried, it was beautiful.

It was also almost the last thing he said to her. They moved into this cute little place furnished with all the prizes, which Anthony had talked about for weeks before the wedding, and that was that. He wasn't mean to her or anything, he just didn't have much time for her. Said he had to keep his energies high for Jai Alai, if he didn't, he would start losing instead of winning, and what would happen to them then? He was nice enough to her, he kissed her on her birthday and they had breakfast together every morning, which is to say she got up and fixed it and he ate it and left, and if she was not awake by the time he came home after the Jai Alai fronton, it didn't matter much.

She could have lived with it too, she thought, she had her job, she had her little home with the checkered curtains in the kitchen and the darling breakfast china with the rooster pattern on it and the cutest little orange bathroom set, a johnny cover with an orange-and-white checkered ruffle on it and a brush holder colored to match. She had her identity as a person in her own right, with her job and bowling on Tuesdays and Thursdays and lunches with the girls, she tatted dresser-top covers for herself and all her girlfriends while watching television on weekends and she already had her husband, she would never again suffer the humiliation of going to the Heartsease Singles Club.

The trouble was, she was going to be expected to meet the public soon and account for her first year of marriage and all the dandy prizes she had been given, up to and including Anthony, and she was worried to death. What happened was, the "Get Rich Television Wedding Show" had scheduled a First Wedding Anniversary Reunion, the invitation came in the same mail as this flier in a pink envelope marked CONFIDENTIAL and addressed to: WIFE OF OCCUPANT. It was, she would decide later, like fate. Here was the embossed card with the network logo, inviting her and Anthony to return to the show along with everybody else that got married in that same week on the show last June, and not only had her marriage deteriorated, but Anthony had deteriorated too. He was so fat she was ashamed to be seen with him, and she knew he wasn't getting fat on her Pop Tarts or her Sara Lee, any more than he was getting his sunburn on her balcony. What's more, he was growing a terrible beard that looked like hog bristle when she could bring herself to look at it, and felt like a wire brush on the few occasions when she and Anthony were close enough to touch. In addition to which he had bought a motorcycle cap with a Nazi emblem on it and a lot of other unusual-looking clothes but when she tried to ask him about it he pushed her face into her neck with one indifferent hand and said a person couldn't stay in mini-bikes forever, it was time to start thinking big.

She knew he had a motorcycle stashed somewhere, she just didn't know where, and she rather imagined he was part of the bike gang that buzzed babies in the park, they had nicked one last week and it was only a matter of time . . . How was she going to explain this change to Alphonse Hinkle, the smiling master of ceremonies on the "Get Rich Television Wedding Show?" How was she going to go out there in front of them all and let the whole world see that the Anthony she had brought back to them after one year of wedded bliss was not the Anthony who had said *I do?* How was she going to explain this to the orchestra and the crew and the nationwide television audience and how was she going to put a good face on the way Anthony looked? Furthermore, whose fault was it anyway? She had the lingering suspicion that they would all blame her. After all, her mother used to say, a man doesn't have to go out to a restaurant when he gets good cooking right in his own house. She knew this was probably symbolic but dammit, she was not going to take the rap for this. If he refused to go it might be better, but unless they turned up together, they were never going to get the Anniversary bonus of a microwave oven and food processor/disposal combination to say nothing of the bonus trip to Tijuana or the matching fur coats.

So the advertisement that came in the same mail with the invitation to the "Get Rich Television Wedding Show" Anniversary Production was like the answer to a maiden's prayer.

MARITAL PROBLEMS? the flier read.

SOLVE THEM WITH THE MARRIAGE BUG

(Transistorized Troubleshooter Ends Upset on the Spot)

In the picture the product looked a little like a Stick Up, one of those things people put around to dissolve odors in trouble spots, it was the same size and color-keyed, but it cost considerably more. She could have taken a loan on the Datsun but when she went down to the bank she discovered that Anthony had their assets all tied up. Heaven only knew what he had done with the money, it was gone, but she supposed that wasn't too bad because he had all that Jai Alai money he kept stowed in the galvanized mailbox he hid under his side of the bed and locked into the bedroom every time he left the house. Which is how she ended up under the marital bed on her hands and knees in the middle of the night after she got the advertisement, crawling around trying to open the damn box while Anthony slept, and is certainly why she found herself snuffling and scratching and nosing Anthony's hand when he half-woke and reached under the bed to find out what was the matter; it also accounted for the humiliation she had to undergo in order to sneak the money out without waking him, snuffling and licking his hand and pretending to be the dog. The next day, of course, she had to get a dog, and bring it into the breakfast nook along with the Pop Tarts before he came blundering out of the bathroom; she made it, but it was close.

She sprang the invitation and the brand-new Marriage Bug on him at the same time. The bug was a secret of course, but she felt better just having it in the house. The minute the package came she opened it with lightning fingers, and without even pausing to read the instructions, put one unit under the breakfast table and the other, after considerable thought, on the doorframe above the door to their bedroom which, since Anthony was not in the house, was locked. When he came home that night, drunk as he was, he had to listen to her reading the invitation to the anniversary show and tired and cross as he was, he had to look at the card the producers had sent and run his finger over the embossed network logo at the top. He waited for her to finish and then yawned and scratched his belly. "Is that all?"

"Yes, Anthony," she said patiently, "that's all for now."

She supposed it was going to take a couple of days for her new appliances to work. The next morning she watched for change over the breakfast table, after all, she had stuck the thing right under the place where Anthony always put his plate, but if there was any difference it was that Anthony had shaved, and not for her. That night when he came in drunk she watched for signs of change but if there were any, it was in the new tenderness with which he counted the money into the galvanized mailbox on his lap; he was a little more intent than usual, that was all. As it turned out this was because he had missed the five hundred dollars she had pilfered to buy the Marriage Bug in the first place, and if the one she had stuck above the bedroom door was working at all it was not working very well because he grabbed her by the scruff of the neck and shook her until she told him where it was; she said she had spent it on stock in Corporated Foods because after all they made most of the family dinners in those plastic freezer pouches, and he let her go just as soon as she confessed and promised him she'd pay it back.

When Anthony got up the next morning and knocked her around

for putting raspberry Pop Tarts into the toaster oven for him instead of the apple ones, his favorites, she went back and read the directions for the Marriage Bug.

DO NOT BE DISHEARTENED BY TEMPORARY SETBACKS

the folder said, underneath a picture of the appliance put into place and properly activated. It went on reassuringly:

WAIT FOR RESULTS.

That was all very well, she thought, but the anniversary show was less than a week away and it was going to take that long for the bruise on her face to fade, and she was still going to have to put on a layer of Cover Girl before she could face the public at that. Anthony seemed to be getting worse, not better, she had put five hundred dollars into this and so far it had given her nothing but grief. She wandered into the breakfast nook and got down on her hands and knees under the table and looked up at the thing, the case was yellow, to go with her café curtains and her breakfast set. She was not certain, but she thought she saw a few lines of tiny, tiny writing on the top. She ran her fingers over it and there was indeed something there, in raised lettering, but she was afraid to disturb the thing so she could bring it out and read it, she might sever the connection, and besides, it was time to go to work. When she got home she would take a flashlight and climb up on a chair and read the lettering on the Marriage Bug above the bedroom door, she thought, but there was going to be an office inspection this morning and she could not be late.

The girls in the typing pool were more than a little snotty about the bruises on her forehead but she just told them about the anniversary show and on the lunch hour she went out and bought her costume for it, an iridescent jumpsuit with spaghetti straps and a pair of Golden Spikes to match and they shut up. When she got home, she pulled a chair over to the doorway and was all ready to climb up and look at the lettering on the Marriage Bug when she heard a motorcycle underneath the window and in the next second the front door opened and Anthony was home.

"Anthony," she said, pushing the chair aside in nervous haste, "What are you doing home?"

He looked at her in confusion. "Damned if I know. What's to eat?"

So she forgot about the lettering for the moment, and went into the kitchen and started a couple of quick-thaw pouches of creamed turkey and broccoli, humming because she thought maybe, just maybe, her new product had started to work.

Of course it hadn't, really. No sooner had they sat down to supper than the buzzer rang and when she went to the door she was struck speechless by the large, amorphous gang clustered outside: boys, girls, people who were neither, all in motorcycle garb. One of them separated herself from the mass at large and faced up to Avis, saying, "Can Anthony come out?"

She was all set to say "Certainly not" and slam the door on them when Anthony rose to his feet and pushed her aside like so many yards of beaded curtain and hurried out.

She finished her creamed turkey and broccoli alone, crying into the cute little cup with the rooster pattern that she had intended for his after-dinner Instakaf. Then she pulled out that chair and climbed up to look at the Marriage Bug planted above the bedroom door (which was still locked because he was out) and read the raised lettering:

IN CASE OF MALFUNCTION
TWIST CAP

What would happen? She did not know, but she thought she could guess. So what if that was what it was, a self-destruct that included her and Anthony, what difference did it make? She didn't care, she'd had enough. If the damn thing didn't work one way she was going to make it work another; she had put down five hundred dollars and the anniversary show was only three days away; she was going to get there and get those prizes and if she did not . . . If worst came to worst she was going to find the manufacturer of the Marriage Bug and firebomb the office and get her money back.

Anthony was so cute when he came in that night, he actually nuzzled her before he curled up with his galvanized mailbox and his extra-large stack of winnings, that she decided to give him one more chance.

She got up ninety minutes early the next morning, and stood back from the vibrator bed in which Anthony still lay mounded, sleeping, and considered him. He was just as fat as he'd ever been, she thought, the stubble on his heavy jaw was growing back thicker and blacker than ever, the anniversary show was two days away but if she could just get him to shave and find a proper suit for him that fit, or that she could at least get buttoned across the middle of his middle, if she could only get him to talk and nod or at least smile in the right places, it might still be all right. She went into the bathroom and combed out her hair and applied half a jar of Cover Girl and more lipstick than she needed. She flipped a pretty peignoir on over her nightie and fluffed up her hair with a girlish hand before she went into the kitchenette.

Today was going to be special, she thought, they would start with a Pop Tart buffet, three different kinds, all heated nicely and cut in halves so he could pick and choose. She would try and he would try, they would have a meeting of the minds and then they would be ready to face Alphonse Hinkle smiling, they would bring home all the anniversary prizes and then some—they could even win the extra fifty thousand dollars that went to the Best Couple of the Year. Underneath the table the Marriage Bug was waiting; she touched it and imagined she could feel it humming. Yes, she thought, today was the day, she would get her money's worth and things would start looking up.

Trouble was, Anthony tripped over the dog on his way out of the bedroom, and he was cross and not too thrilled when he got to the table and saw the little platter of Pop Tarts, all neatly cut in half. At least he spoke to her.

"What happened to the Pop Tarts?"

"I made a buffet," she said with her best smile. "I thought you could choose, you know, between all the different kinds?"

"You know I hate Pop Tarts," he said, and swept them off the plate in a single stroke.

"Oh Anthony." What if she cried? She sniffled once or twice.

"You got a cold?"

She sighed. "I got a pain in the neck."

"You're the pain in the neck."

"Are we going to fight?" She thought: *Maybe this is it.* "If we'd ever fight, Anthony, at least we could, ah, open a dialogue, like they say in the magazines?" Her heart was fluttering. She put her whole self into it. "If we had a fight we could kiss and make up."

"I hate Tang, too," he said, as if she hadn't even spoken.

"Anthony, what's become of our marriage?" All he had to say was, what marriage, and they could begin the dialogue.

"I got to go," he said. "I'm late to work."

All right, Anthony, last chance. "You going to the show with me?" She reached under the table and touched the Marriage Bug.

He barely looked over his shoulder. "What show?"

"Ok for you, Anthony," she said, and she gave the cap to the Marriage Bug a savage twist. "This is it."

What did he care? He just kept on walking out; he didn't even bother to ask her, "What's what?" He just kept on walking and then, to her positive amazement, he simply fell into a dozen pieces that rolled off each other, head and neck first, followed by left shoulder, right shoulder, belly, the rest, Anthony disassembling; all the parts tumbled into various corners of the room, and lay inert.

There wasn't any mess; there wasn't even any blood. All there was was Anthony in a dozen different pieces, quiet for the time being, mercifully quiet, and on his way out of her life. She got a plastic garbage bag and started gathering him up. Disposal was going to be a problem, she thought, but if she had to, she would cope, it was a mere detail because she was already feeling better about everything. Things were definitely looking up. She would make up some story to tell Alphonse Hinkle and then . . .

She had just about decided the incinerator chute would be the best place, she could stuff him down one piece at a time, when the parts of Anthony all quietly deflated with a hissing sound and she was left with little more mess than there was after she had eaten her dinner of frozen creamed turkey and broccoli out of the disposable plastic pouch. The Marriage Bug worked after all, it was a sensation. She had her money's worth. She put what was left in the trash compactor without a qualm and then, because it seemed appropriate, said a few words as she threw the switch.

"It's been fun, Anthony, but you should have paid me more mind."

She wore her new iridescent jumpsuit with the spaghetti straps to the Anniversary Gala and Alphonse Hinkle praised her for bravery in the face of her, how was it he put it, her tragic loss. Avis just turned a bright smile to the cameras, confident that the Cover Girl had indeed covered all the bruises, and thanked him and the producers and the studio audience for all their kindness and especially for the black Ford Galaxie which seemed appropriate to her newly widowed state. She already had an invitation to be on the pilot of the "Get Rich Newly Widowed Television Show," which Mr. Hinkle was also going to emcee because it was not really a conflict of interest situation, it gave a sense of continuity, and she felt fine standing up there while the audience applauded, for the first time in one entire year she felt really good.

"Avis, you've been an inspiration to us all," Alphonse Hinkle said while the band played and the studio audience threw white roses supplied by the management. "Tell me honey, if it's not too painful, do you think you'll ever want to get married again?"

"I don't think so Alphonse," she said when the applause had subsided, and as she said the next words they became forever true. "Things were so perfect with Anthony, I wouldn't want to try my luck."

Alumni Fund

Dear Classmate:

You have heard of the gift that keeps on giving. Well today I am writing to call your attention to a little-known part of the university that keeps on asking and unfortunately never receives because your kind donations are being plowed into the new gym or used to clean the ivy out of the mortar before it undermines the memorial arch.

While the rest of you have been going about the business of the world, distinguishing yourselves as wizards of finance and captains of industry and making money, one or two of your classmates have stayed behind here at the old alma mater keeping the home fires burning, Keigwin in chemistry and myself in English.

Naturally I am entertained by your constant attentions to me *vis à vis* the Class Gift Fund, keep those cards and letters coming because it makes a person feel remembered, and if I can't afford to sign up for the reunion weekend I would love to have one of those funny hats. I was especially grateful for the information, written in your treasurer's own hand at the bottom of the reunion communication, that some benevolent classmate has paid this year's premium on the life insurance policy taken out in my name, but on the other hand I resent the additional suggestion that I send along one or two dollars, whatever I can afford, just to help make our class one hundred percent for our twentieth, a note I find both condescending and insulting.

I don't want you to think I don't have the two dollars, of course I have it, but at the moment I happen to owe it in several different places. While the rest of you have been out forging bucks and getting your offices carpeted, Keigwin and I have been teaching your children and others like you at a salary that I suspect you would consider risible.

Which is not to say we don't enjoy it, for the time your children are in our classes we all manage to pretend that they may graduate to become latter-day Pasteurs or Miltons, it keeps them happy and us from despair. We are even able to maintain an illusion of power because it is we who decide whether they are going to pass or fail.

On the other hand, we have children of our own to feed which is increasingly difficult toward the end of the month, especially in view of the fact that for reasons which should be apparent the bank has just ceased to think of me as a Favorite Person, at least until I pay back the three thousand dollars. The neighbors' garden is seeing us through handsomely at the moment but I do anticipate difficulty this winter.

Which brings me to the point. I'm just as sorry as you are that our class won't be a hundred percent this year, at least not unless one of you wants to cough up the two dollars in my name, but I do have an alternative suggestion that you might find amusing. What if each of you forwarded a dollar or two— whatever you can afford—to me at the above address?

Just to keep me a hundred percent.

> Yours in '58
> Samuel J. Winston, Associate
> Professor of English

September 15, 198–

Dear Alumnus:

You are one of a privileged group of alumni selected this year to receive this special communication. Your previous generosity has not gone unnoticed, but what are you receiving in return? Heretofore even your greatest contributions have been diffused through the sieve of the Class Gift Fund or the Building Fund or Annual Giving, all that money you have so generously sent has gotten mixed up with everybody else's money with the net result that not one of you can come back to the college of your youth and find so much as a water fountain bearing your name.

I am offering you an opportunity to rectify this with a unique approach to university giving, and with this mailing I want to introduce you to the concept of a gift you can keep control of because it is targeted, generosity with a personal touch.

What better memorial than a professorship that bears your name? Given to a professor who will write you once a month and remember you at Christmas? One who will open his home to you when ever you return for an alumni bash? You can have immediate and visible results by endowing a professor's car. Or his house (at the moment it's not in very good repair but it has style and I think you'll like it). What greater joy than a gift which goes on giving to a recipient who goes on thanking? What greater pleasure than grateful letters and phone calls filled with personal news, or perhaps you would prefer a glowing verse tribute, a lasting memorial to an honored patron?

Let me explain . . .

Sept. 15, 198–

Dear Colleague:

At this crucial time, with the matter of your tenure still pending, I'd like to call to your attention an opportunity you may have overlooked . . .

Lecture, 9 A.M. Sept. 15, 198–

"Now class, I note that several of you are with me for the second or third term in your college career, which makes me think I must be selling something you are interested in buying. You are, on the other hand, failing to get the most out of the experience your parents are paying so much to obtain for you and the reasons are clear. I see very little of that tuition money, and because of the night job at the Holiday Inn to make ends meet, the time I can afford to give you is limited at best.

"The way things are set up now I am seldom able to come to the front door at night to discuss your personal problems or why you only got a C, at least not for what I am getting paid, as it doesn't even cover a forty-hour week, much less sixty or seventy.

"With this in mind I am prepared to make a series of offers that will enhance your learning experience and free me to spend more time with you. First I would like to institute a simple rate scale for extra lecture sessions and individual or group conferences outside class time, and I think if there is no objection I am going to extend that to all those little personal comments you expect to find written in the margins of your papers, what about, say, twenty-five cents apiece for those, plus a dollar for the page-long summary at the bottom of the paper. I will add that there will be a flat rate for receiving night phone calls about those extensions on your papers and I would like to state furthermore that although I am incorruptible I am also desperate so there may or may not be a tangible relationship between your end-of-term grades and your pledged contributions to the Samuel J. Winston fund which I am instituting today to put you in touch with the larger concept of university giving, and those of you who are hard-up financially will be welcome to come over and work in the yard.

"There will be no extra charge for personal comments made during class time, but you must be prepared to make arrangements in advance for any notes put in your box or suggested extra reading and you can begin to book now for my conversations with your mothers or fathers at the annual Parents' Day reception upcoming in October.

"Conference bookings can be made as you leave the room at the end of the period but right now I would appreciate it if you'd start those pledge cards moving up toward the front, and after they are tallied we can begin."

The Revenge of the Senior Citizens
A Novella

"It's hell being old."

Even though they were alone in the bathtub-shaped rest area at the south end of the Ebb Tide Mall, the man sat down right next to Marian, who tried not to think of herself as old. She kept herself nicely and she looked very pretty today in the blue cotton she had put on to come to the mall, well put-together in the neat white espadrilles with the snappy matching pocketbook. Mother would have died to see her out in public without stockings, but poor Mother had been dead for more than fifty years.

When she didn't answer he tapped the cigar box he was carrying lightly and said, "Did you ever get the feeling it's all passing you by?"

He looked like a nice old man just about her age, but you never knew. He could be a wolf. He had a pleasant expression and he was natty and well-kept in the yellow seersucker Bermudas and the crisp white shirt, but she did not know what was in the cigar box or what was on his mind. He set the box down on the moulded Permastone seating arrangement and began sliding closer. She slid away.

"I mean look at those people." He made a wide gesture at the young, who swarmed past without even a glance for the old man and the old lady sitting in the rest area. "We might as well be dead."

She stifled a gasp but did not respond. He had the kind of face that made a person want to confide, but they had not been properly introduced.

"Do you come here often?"

"My daughter is in that store right there and she is coming back for me in just a minute." Marian said it as a precautionary measure. He would not dare try anything now. God knew when Sally would be back but one of the first things Marian had learned as a young lady was never to speak to strangers, and the second was never to let the stranger know you were alone. It was funny, she thought, or was it only sad to know that she had always been a perfect lady, she had taken everything Mother had said seriously and tried to pass it on to the girls. She had done everything properly and yet here she was, just as lonely as if she had done it all wrong. Now she had offended this nice man, who was picking up his cigar box as if to go.

"I mean, I promised her I would wait," she said quickly.

He put the cigar box down.

"She's very thoughtful."

He tilted his head. "Sure she is."

"She didn't want me to get tired following her around."

"They don't like being followed and you know it," he said.

This was true, but nobody ever said it aloud. "Oh dear."

"It's true."

It was like being marooned, she thought, as the tide of shoppers broke and flowed around the rest area, hundreds of young people in a hurry. They went on their way without so much as a glance for the two senior citizens risking rheumatism or hemorrhoids or worse on the beige Permastone. She could starve to death right here or freeze to the bench; this gentleman could make improper advances and nobody would notice. Still what could she do? Sally had made her promise to wait right here until she finished shopping. Marian said, stoutly, "She just left me here for a minute."

"That's what they all say. She's gone for the afternoon."

"Not Sally." How long would Sally take anyway? No telling. She never wanted Marian to see her try things on and she got cross when Marian complained about waiting.

"Mine makes no bones about it. She gives me five and dumps me for the day."

"Your own daughter? You could stay home."

"She says I'd only get in trouble. If you want to know the truth she isn't even in this mall."

"No!"

"She's gone off to the Gulliver Mall, over by the highway? Says the ramps would be too hard on me. If you want to know the truth she hates to see me coming."

"That's terrible."

"That's the way things are."

"Not for me," Marian said hastily. "Sally takes very good care of me."

"My name is Victor Wimsatt."

"How do you do?"

"If you want to know the truth my back is killing me."

He looked all right to her. He had been attractive in his day and he had that smile . . . "I'm Marian Enright." This sounded too naked. "Mrs. Burton Enright."

Naturally he saw right through her with those clear blue eyes. "You're another widow. Otherwise you wouldn't be stuck here alone."

"He died in the war. At least I think he did. Never a day goes by that I don't think of him."

"Elva only shuffled off four years ago. She was a bad cook and I never liked her much but I still miss her."

A tough-looking old man in khakis went by with a half-salute for Victor, who acknowledged it with a nod and kept looking after him, obviously thinking about something else now. "Burton was very considerate," she said, to bring him back. "Who was that?"

"A friend. Sometimes a bunch of us get together and try to plan . . ."

"Plan?"

"Yes," he said, not answering. "I still miss Elva. Just another body, in the house? You know, when you came home and said hello there was somebody to answer back. I hated being alone, but . . ."

"I did it for a long time."

". . . it was better than living at my daughter's."

"I live at my daughter's too." She wondered why this made her stomach sour.

"She made me come and live with her, damned if I know why."

Marian was remembering all those conversations with the children, how they sold her house right out from under her, got rid of half her things. "Probably she was worried about you."

"That's what they say. If you want to know the truth, they can't stand having me around."

"Don't say that! Please don't."

"Want to know what I've got in the box?"

"Why of course not. It's none of my business."

"Well I've got a gun in here."

"No you don't." She put her hands over her mouth.

"Oh yes I do. Want to know what I'm going to do with it?"

"Not really." She looked over her shoulder anxiously. Where was Sally? The girl was always going off and leaving her, sometimes for hours, it was inconsiderate. She didn't know whether he had a gun or not but he was worrying her to death. "No, I wouldn't."

"I'll tell you what I have half a mind to do," he said anyway. "I have half a mind to go to the movies and sit through as many features as I can afford, which is about three on what she gives me, and then go into the men's room and shoot myself."

"Oh no!"

"If you want to know the truth my life is not worth living."

She put her hands to her eyes.

"Neither is yours, and you know it."

"That's not true!"

"Of course it's true. So that's what I have half a mind to do." He centered the box on his knees and put his palms on it. "But with the other half of my mind, well, I'm working on a plan."

"If you're going to kill yourself, I'm going to have to call the police."

"Relax, little lady." He looked away from her to acknowledge the greeting of a sturdy-looking woman with a frizzy grey permanent, who tipped him a wink and patted her shoulder bag as she went by. "Relax, I said I'm working on a plan."

"Mr. Wimsatt, it's really been nice talking to you," Marian said nervously, "it's been nice talking to you and I really would like to stay but I . . . I promised my daughter I would meet her at the central fountain, I promised her I would meet her there just about now."

"You promised you would meet her here and you know it. Now relax, Mrs. Enright, I promise not to trouble you. What I want you to do is . . ." He lowered his voice and looked around sharply, to be certain they weren't being overheard. "I want you to consider what I have to say to you."

"I'm sorry, I don't feel well . . ."

"Of course you don't. Your life is going downhill. Admit it, Mrs. Enright, isn't your life going downhill?"

"No, I just don't feel well," Marian said.

"And it's happening more and more often. Look where they put you, stashed in some back room with all your things. Do you want to know why they stash you in the back room?"

"It's a very nice room."

"They keep you there so they won't have to look at you."

"I make my own clothes. I go on trips to see my other children."

"And they go all funny when they see you coming."

"I'm their mother!"

"My dear, that's just the point."

It was a long time since anyone had called her dear. "Mr. Wimsatt!"

"And if you don't know why they go all funny, let me lay it out."

"No."

"They go all funny because they see the future written on us. When we walk in they see the failure of their bodies, all those wrinkles and punky hearts, distended veins, they see the short sight and the hard of hearing, the not being able to make it up the stairs."

"Don't say that."

"When they see us they see the end. No wonder they are scared of us."

"They're not!"

"They hate us for making them feel old."

"But that's terrible." She gave in to that strange, liquid feeling that overtook her when she was upset. Now she wondered if her daughter Sally felt it too.

"I bet they have a nice place lined up for you to go."

The folders, the papers they wanted her to sign; she fought off panic. "My daughter thinks I'd enjoy being with people who share the same interests."

"Like elastic bandages and ostomy bags."

"Like shuffleboard, and bridge."

"Like dying."

"Television. Nice music. Like golf."

"I bet you never played golf."

"She wants me to be comfortable," Marian said anxiously.

"She wants you in an old persons' hatch."

"Retirement community."

"She can't wait to get rid of you."

Marian was agitated now. "She wants me to be well taken care of."

"That's just the point. Out of sight, out of mind." He snapped the lid of the box. "All those places? Just simple disposal methods, if you take my meaning. Me, I have a choice. I can either beat them to it, or —I can use this gun to get the jump on them."

"I'm sorry, but that's crazy."

"You ought to get out more, talk to people. Then you'd know how crazy I am. Look at it this way. The young don't need us any more. They don't even want us."

"That's an awful thing to say."

"It's true. We're just a drain on them. So if we won't go quietly, if they can't move us out—they're going to have to look for other ways." He let his voice drop. "You know there is a conspiracy."

"I wish you would go away."

"It's either us or them."

"I didn't ask you to sit with me."

"You didn't stop me, either. Admit it. It's true. They are trying to get rid of us." He pounded the polished Permastone, which gave back no sound. "They'll do anything. Getting you upset, in hopes you'll throw a clot? All those airplane crashes, and they keep sending you on trips. Surprise changes in your medication. Drafts. And some of them . . ."

She was shaking her head, sliding away from him.

"Some of them," he said, sliding after her, "some of them will try anything."

Oh *God.* She had slid to the closed end of the oval, where she was more or less stuck. She would have to make a U-turn with her rear end before she could slide the other way and get away from him. Meanwhile where was Sally, who had dumped her here? She had been in that store forever. Where was the wretched girl? How many days had Marian wasted in places just like this one? What if Sally had dumped her here and run away? She began calling. "Sally?"

He just went on in a chilling whisper. "Faulty wiring. Operations you don't need. Putting your heater right next to the bathtub. Ultrasonic devices."

She started. "What?"

"Ultrasonic devices. Those little things that sit in your kitchen and glow, so you'll know they're working?"

Sally had one. The literature said it covered an area of a thousand feet. "But those are for roaches."

"So they *say*," he finished with a look of pure triumph.

Marian was distracted by a figure approaching, a grim, middle-aged harridan with sagging breasts and sagging shoulders, a mouth that looked like a snapping turtle's, no lips and all bite. Poor old thing, she thought, and in the next beat recognized her daughter. When had Sally stopped being a girl? Marian did not want to think about it. "Oh Sally, there you are." She smiled graciously. "I'd like you to meet Mr. Wimsatt."

If Sally heard she did not slow her progress. "I told you to stay where I put you. Where have you been? I've been looking for you for an hour."

"I've been right here."

"No you haven't. If you had, I would have seen you. I left you in the rest area outside Penney's, remember?"

Had she? Marian didn't think so, but she could not remember. "I've been right here the whole time, honey, I . . ."

"If you can't stay put I'm going to have to . . ." Sally's mind closed on what she was going to have to do and her mouth snapped shut.

Victor Wimsatt was whispering, "Been experiencing strange headaches since she got that thing? Nausea? Dizziness?"

"Oh please," she said to both of them.

"Just watch these." Sally dumped her packages.

"Have they mixed up your medication?"

"But Sally, I haven't eaten."

"Keep tripping over things in the dark?"

"Just wait here."

"Sally, I'm *hung*ry."

"Oh here." Sally slapped something on the bench and walked away, saying something Marian could not catch. Why did the children always have to mumble?

"What?" She blinked rapidly. "What did she say?"

"Typical. Just typical. She told you not to talk to strangers."

"I'm so sorry, I . . ."

"She left you a quarter. She said it was for lunch."

"Oh I'm so embarrassed." Marian hid her face for just a moment. Then, because she knew he was still watching her, and because she knew he hadn't missed a thing: not the edge to Sally's voice, not her rudeness, not the way she treated her own mother, she said, "I hope you understand she isn't always that way, she's been under a strain lately . . ."

He touched her hand. It was the last straw.

"Please don't cry."

"I'm not crying," she said, pulling out a handkerchief and mopping under her glasses. "I . . . I guess I am." She just went ahead and let her face crumple because he was patting her hand and saying "there there" and after years of widowhood this was an enormous luxury. "Oh Mr. Wimsatt, I don't ordinarily . . ."

"We all ought to do more of it," he said. "Good for us. Now if I leave you here are you going to be all right?"

"I've had to be all right for a long time, Mr. Wimsatt. Ten minutes more won't make any . . ." Oh Lord, maybe he was running out on her. Better to pretend it did not matter.

"Hold this. I'm going to buy both of us a decent sandwich."

It was the cigar box. She set it on the bench close enough so nobody would steal it but not so close that she had to touch it. She was afraid to open the lid.

Waiting for Mr. Wimsatt, whom she had begun to think of as Victor, Marian got out her compact and fixed her face. She had long since stopped trying to figure out why keeping up her looks was still so important to her even though she was, after all, a grandmother, but she knew it was. Her insides were still quivering and she realized now that this was partly the effect of his unexpected kindness and partly the fear that he would be swept away in the tide of shoppers and she would never see him again. What if he was just a passing thing? What if he came back and tried to take her pocketbook, or sell her worthless stocks? What if Victor was a wolf? What was she going to do, one woman alone? Well she had been alone for a long time, she thought, and with an uneven sigh touched her eyes with her hankie and put it back in her pocketbook and snapped it shut. She would sit here and wait for her own daughter that didn't even want her but had to take her home anyway because it was her duty. She would smile pleasantly so everybody would know she had not been abandoned, but was busy waiting. She would show the world that she was not pitiful or frightening, she was just one more nice old lady among all the other nice old ladies who whiled away the empty days on benches in parks or in department-store cafeterias or in the rest areas in malls, who had no more life than coming in and going out until they got too sick to go out, after which there would only be staying in. Yet this strange Mr. Wimsatt had raised a little crop of hopes and stirred a web of emotions she had forgotten. He had been nice to her, he had touched her hand.

He had mumbled something about a plan.

A plan. What plan was there, except to get through the remaining years with the least fuss? What could any of them hope for, at their age? He said he had a gun in the cigar box, he said he was going to shoot himself, or else . . . What did he mean, or else?

She was going to give him five more minutes to come back, and then . . .

Did she dare?

Would she?

Yes. She would give him five more minutes and then she was going to open the lid.

"I was going to buy falafel but I didn't know whether sprouts agreed with you."

Her heart leaped up. "You came back!"

"Little lady, you knew I would."

So they sat there celebrating their new friendship with chicken salad sandwiches and milk in half-pint cartons, Marian feeling fresh and pretty as a debutante and Mr. Wimsatt joyful at first, almost frivolous, but growing more and more serious as they folded the sandwich papers and crumpled the milk cartons and put them neatly into the sack. When they had finished eating he said, quietly, "Your daughter isn't very nice to you, is she?"

Marian blushed. "She does her best."

"Call it what you want. You're too nice to be treated that way."

She put her hands to her cheeks to cool them. "Flatterer."

"No, just being realistic. We're all in the same predicament. Nice people, who are being pushed out of the way." He cleared his throat with an awkward rattle. "Well, Mrs. Enright . . ."

"Marian."

"Well, Marian, I wanted you to be the first to know."

"I beg your pardon?"

"I've definitely decided I'm not going to kill myself."

"Oh Mr. Wimsatt, I . . ."

"Victor." He reached for her hand. "I have something to live for now."

She bridled. "Whatever do you mean?"

"You know I mean you. So I am not going to lie down quietly and let them carry me away. I'm going to fight back. They're not going to get me with their roach boxes or anything else."

"You don't really believe it's the roach boxes."

"They'll try anything. Have you ever seen a dead roach around one of those things?"

"I guess I haven't, but still . . ." She might as well bring all her doubts out in the open. "How could a little thing like a roach box cause us any harm? They don't even make any noise."

"That's just the point. It's something they're doing to us with ultrasound. It's pitched so high it doesn't even bother them. I have a scientist friend who can explain. You know, when you get older, things that didn't used to bother you can start to bother you?"

"Lord knows that's the truth. Drafts, certain kinds of food . . ." She had not been herself for months, but she had blamed this on Sally's cooking, which was none too good. What if her daughter was getting at her in other ways?

"The roach boxes are pitched so high they don't bother young people, but if your ears are sensitive at all—do you begin to see?"

Marian thought about Sally and her husband Albert, all the petty unkindnesses and little hardships that had piled up in the years since she had moved in with them, about the lonely evenings in the TV room, while they were somewhere else, ignoring her, about their accumulated ill will . . . "I'm afraid I do."

"So it's either us or them," he said. "Are you all right?"

"I just want to be quiet for a while."

This time he was gone for a half hour, in which Marian tried to assemble her thoughts. She was dimly aware that Victor was talking to the stocky woman she had seen before, who leaned against the pillar outside the hairdresser's opposite and conferred seriously. Later she saw him in conversation with a pair of men she didn't recognize and still later she saw him say something to the man in khakis he had greeted right after they met, and when he caught her looking he waved and Marian waved back. After a time he came back to the rest area and reclaimed the cigar box, which she had been protecting for him.

"So it's set for tomorrow," he said.

"Victor, I still don't know what you're . . ."

He cut her off. "You might as well know, little lady, I didn't sit down next to you by accident."

"Why Victor!"

"I picked you out," he said, grinning like a boy.

"I've been depressed most of the time, lately, you might as well know. We keep talking about making a plan, but I kept thinking, who do I have to live for, what's the point of bothering with a plan? Then I saw you and . . . So you see, you made up my mind for me."

"I did no such thing," she said giddily, both pleased and disturbed.

"It could have gone either way this morning, you know, go into the bathroom at the movies, take the gun out of the box, or get it together, as the kids put it, find a better way to use the gun."

"You're not going to shoot anybody . . ."

"Not unless I have to." He saw her troubled expression. "No, I would never shoot anybody, I promise. No. But this thing isn't going to work unless we all come armed."

"What isn't going to work? What thing?" Her heart was pounding so hard now that she was afraid for her health but it was a good kind of pounding, a good excitement, that she remembered from early childhood, the sense of her whole life running on ahead.

"Now settle down, please. That's it." He took both her hands and held them down until he had her quiet. "Now I'd like you to listen very carefully. You don't have to make up your mind about this thing right now. All you have to do is sit quietly and listen to me. Just listen, you don't even have to say anything when I'm through. Just go home, think about it, and then tomorrow either you'll come back or you won't come back."

She closed her eyes in the short silence that followed, and felt herself floating, about to fly up to the vaulted ceiling, anchored only by Victor's strong hands and then by his voice, as he resumed.

"What I'm asking you to do is take a chance with us. I saw the way your daughter dumped you here, I heard what she said when she left you to go shopping."

"No you didn't."

"I was standing right over there, behind the urn? I saw her and I heard what she said to you. I know what my daughter said and I know what my friends' children said. Now we have all of us decided we don't have to stand for that kind of treatment, and so we're not going to."

She still had her eyes closed. She was aware that Victor had removed one of his hands from hers and opened the cigar box. He took her hand and settled it on the object inside. She gasped and her eyes flew open at the touch of cold steel.

"You see, my dear, it's time to make a stand. We're going to meet down here tomorrow, myself and a group of like-minded people, and I'd be very happy if you decided to meet with us too. No, no, don't say anything now. Don't do anything but listen, and then go home and think." He stood up then and tucked the cigar box under his arm. "I'm going to the movies now, Marian, I'm just going to walk away and never look back. If you're with us, why then I'll see you down here tomorrow, same time, same station, and we'll . . . we'll start our life."

"Wait!"

"If you're with me, bring your friends. Goodbye, my dear."

That *dear* again! "Goodbye . . ."

"And tell them to come armed." He looked just a little like Gary Cooper, walking away. He would not look back to see her wave.

The first thing she did when she got home was sneak in the kitchen and inspect her daughter's roach box. It was sitting next to the toaster, glowing dully. The light, she was told, was to let the homeowner know it was working; what the roaches heard was pitched too high for the human ear. If this was true, why did she have a strange buzzing in her ears; all the tissues were drying out with age, she had been told this by the doctor, and she was sure they were all rattling now. The ultrasonic device was harmless to humans, all the literature said so, but why did her hand tremble as she touched it, and why did she have this blinding pain behind the eyes? What was it doing to the inside of her head? It was not enough to make a stand on and she knew it, but it was going to have to do. One way or another, she was ready for a change, she was ready to face up to her life and make it different.

Feeling the warmth in the object, the slight vibration, she realized it was not so much the roach box they were rebelling against as what it signified: the wishes and efforts of the young to get shut of them, the need for a change. Yes, she thought, remembering the pressure of Victor's fingers, we're going to do something about our lives.

We are already doing it.

Victor and I.

It did not take her much time to convince her bridge group. When they were together they could laugh and forget how old they were. They all loved a party, and were ready for anything. Cecelia and Maud agreed to empty their bank accounts and bring traveler's checks in addition to whatever might do for a weapon; even Rebecca agreed, and of the four girls, she was the most conservative.

That nice Mr. Messer who lived with his children across the street could hardly contain himself. He was a retired postal employee, tall and thin, and he walked with a slight slouch, but when she spoke to him out front he said, "I've been waiting for this."

She said, without conviction, "That's wonderful."

"You might as well know, my hands are lethal weapons."

His hands were skinny and speckled. "What?"

"I'm trained in the martial arts."

"Lord, I hope we aren't called upon to do anything like that."

"There's no telling what we might be called upon to do."

Sobered by his enthusiasm, she went into her own backyard to enlist Mr. Glackens, who kept fit by doing Sally's yard work. He was taking advantage of the cool twilight hours to hoe out a new flower bed. She was aware that she and Mr. Glackens were being watched.

She kept her back to the window where Sally was lingering and lowered her voice.

"My friend says we've got to act now or die. He says there is a conspiracy."

Mr. Glackens was short, stocky, as bald as that old trademark character, what was his name? Mr. Clean. Mr. Glackens was as bald as Mr. Clean. He squinted. "I hate to say this, but you've got some imagination."

"Let me put it this way, Mr. Glackens. My friend thinks it's in the roach things. You know, the sound boxes they all bought?"

His eyes were the color of his faded chambray shirt, and when he widened them, as if that would help him understand what she was trying to tell him, she imagined she could see right through to the back of his head. "What about them?"

"Does your daughter-in-law have one?"

"She has about eight of them." He started to run his fingers through his hair, remembered he didn't have any and grimaced. "After all, this is Florida."

"But the roaches aren't dying."

"You're right. I guess they're not."

She played her hole card. "And you've been having headaches. Getting dizzy. Feeling strange."

"I thought that was just age."

"That's what we all think, but normal people don't have those things. We didn't used to have them. Am I right?"

"Yes ma'am."

"My friend thinks it's them."

"I'll be there." He caught sight of Sally spying from the window and he bent over the flower bed, adding in a low tone, "And armed."

In bed that night, Marian had the uncomfortable feeling that Sally and her husband were on to her. Why else would she and the uncouth Albert come into the Florida room and sit right next to her while she watched TV? They sat there and mumbled, which they knew got on her nerves, and Sally stuffed her with salted TV mix, which the doctor had clearly said was bad for her blood pressure and her digestion too. ("I made it specially, Mother, after all . . .") Later, when their grownup children came by they all retreated to the screen porch, nodding in Marian's direction occasionally and conversing in whispers. That night after everybody went to bed Marian crept down to the kitchen in the dark and unplugged the ultrasonic roach deterrent, but she slept badly and woke with a headache all the same. At breakfast Sally made her eat bacon, which was loaded with sodium, and blueberry pancakes, when she knew what fruit did to Marian's insides, and when Marian asked nicely whether they could go to the mall today Sally had a tantrum.

"Mother, we just went to the mall. Don't you remember?"

"But I didn't get to buy anything."

"You know you can't afford much on a fixed income. Besides, you just spent the check we gave you for your birthday."

Marian said, guiltily, "I just thought a scarf, a new lipstick, something to keep me cheerful."

"Well I would love to but today you're going to the doctor, remember?"

Marian was embarrassed because she had forgotten. "I don't trust that young man. He's only a baby."

"He's the best cardiologist in the city."

"Be that as it may I don't like his manner. He's rude, poking at me that way. Besides, he mumbles, just like everybody else." Marian wished Sally would stop crashing pots so they could have this conversation. She wanted to give her daughter one last chance to be friends and she shouted, over the racket, "It's all right. You don't have to take me."

"That's more like it."

"I'll go on the bus," she said under her breath.

"Go get your bath so you'll be decent for the doctor." If Sally didn't hear it was because she didn't want to hear.

Later Marian would be sorry she had skipped the bath but she was in a hurry. She chose the tailored blue seersucker because it made her look efficient and the Navy espadrilles because they were comfortable and would not show the dirt. She picked out a straw bag big enough to hold Burton's pearl-handled razor and other necessaries like her medications and a can of Mace which she had stolen from Sally's spice shelf in case of armed robbery and kept in her dresser ever since. As it was important to let people know she was a lady even in moments of confrontation, she put on Mother's amethyst brooch and her jeweled watch. On second thought she put in three sets of underthings. She had the idea she would not be coming back here. She tucked in her bankbooks and a nightie, and for the first time in her life she did not make her bed before leaving. She had never been more excited.

What if she got there and he didn't come? The suspense was terrible. She was surprised by the way her heart surged as she got close enough to the rest area to make out his face, and by the way her stomach twisted with jealousy at the sight of Cecelia and Maud from her bridge club. They must have been at the mall even before the doors opened, and they were openly flirting with him.

"Oh Marian, it's you," Cecelia said.

"How did you get here so fast?"

Maud, who looked nice but impractical in her aqua dotted swiss, gave Marian a superior smile. "Cecelia drove us."

"Well you could have given me a ride." She was about to go on: *It isn't fair,* but Victor had turned away from the others as if she were the only person in the rest area.

He approached with his hands outstretched. "You came."

She clasped them. "You knew I would."

"I was counting on you," he said for the group at large.

"Why thank you. Thank you very much." He had changed position so that they were standing side by side now, like . . . she didn't know what. All she thought was: *That will show the girls.*

Within an hour there were thirty of them in the rest area—all of Marian's friends came, including Mr. Messer, who was wearing what appeared to be a safari jacket with a dozen bulging pockets; he jingled as he joined the group sitting on the Permastone bench. Mr. Glackens steamed in like a little tank: round, compact, looking so solid and, well, *homey* in his freshly ironed work shirt that Marian was shocked when he brought out two pistols from his canvas tote. Victor's friends were all somewhat grimmer than hers; they were nicely dressed, but men and women alike entered the rest area like troops entering the trenches, a fact which both surprised and also reassured Marian. She was not certain what Victor was planning but it was apparent that she could count on him. Something would happen soon. It was obvious that he had spent the night making lists. He went around the oval giving instructions to each recruit. When it was Marian's turn she said, "You're so organized."

"Got to start somewhere."

"But yesterday you were . . ."

"Ready to end it all." He handed her a typed slip with an affecting smile. "I guess we both know who I have to thank."

She was to go to the scuba shop and buy spearguns for imaginary twin grandsons. This time yesterday she would have called the security officer and turned him in. Today she would do anything for him.

Moving slowly, looking almost aimless and even a little dotty, Victor's people filtered through the mall. They had all lived too long and gone through too much to be hurried now. With great deliberation, they made withdrawals from the various branch banks and went into the stores to make their purchases. A few went to the lawyers' office in one of the kiosks and executed hastily drafted wills. One at a time the senior citizens returned to the rest area, trying to look as if they had just happened by. Then, handing over parcels, they added to the cache of supplies under the lip of the Permastone bench. Some had bought handguns and others ammunition from the sporting-goods manufacturers; some had come back with spearguns and fishermen's knives, and when they had enough weapons in hand they moved back out and brought in food, up to and including liquid protein supplements. It was like getting ready for an ocean voyage, or maybe a safari, doing as Victor ordered without even knowing how the supplies were going to be used. On an inspiration Marian made an unauthorized side trip to buy all the purple T-shirts from three shops. The colors did not all match but they were close enough. If they were going to be a team then they should have uniforms. She would wait until the time was right and give them to Victor to hand out. She did not know what was going to happen next or even whether Victor knew, but whatever happened, it didn't matter. She was happy now.

When the last shopper had returned and all the purchases were stashed under the oval bench, Victor and the others rolled the heavy smoking stands to the open end of the oval rest area, securing the entrance as if closing the gates to a fort. Then because there wasn't room for everybody on the bench he had his people open camp stools and folding chairs so they could all sit down. Anybody who went by might think it was a tent meeting, some impromptu preacher addressing his flock. When everybody was quiet Victor began.

"You may wonder why I have gathered you together here."

"It's either us or them." Mr. Glackens clamped one fist to his barrel chest. The others muttered assent.

"So it's understood."

Mr. Messer snapped, "Damn right it's understood."

For a minute there Victor faltered and Marian wondered if it was his heart. Instead, she decided later, he had sized up the situation, the weight of the mantle of leadership, and even knowing how hard it was going to be, had decided to go ahead. He might not be getting taller as he spoke but he looked taller to her. "So we are the last bastion," he said. "The last outpost, the last people fighting for last things, and there is not a soul alive who would deny our right to do it." Victor raised his fist.

There were cheers.

"Survival at any cost."

The words passed around the circle like a powerful wind. "Survival at any cost."

"It's either us or them." As she spoke Marian looked over her shoulder uneasily. If the passersby were paying them any mind at all they just averted their eyes and hurried on, as if skirting a TB ward, or a leper colony. Nobody liked to see a gathering of old people because it reminded them of things they did not want to think about. The middle-aged were the worst, skirting the rest area as if old age was something you could catch, like a disease. Maybe it was, she thought. The result was the same. By this time Victor's people and even her friends were rallying, getting a little loud, but they might as well be invisible. Marian realized with a little thrill of excitement that they could probably get away with anything. "No more roach boxes," she said.

Victor took up the litany. "Or changes in the medication."

"Or trips to places you're afraid to go to."

"Or being mumbled at."

"Or being rushed."

"This is the end of the rest home."

"The angiogram."

"The skate at the top of the stairs." Victor lifted his hands for silence and then he said, "Our best weapon is surprise."

"Right," Mr. Messer said. "Take them unawares."

Victor looked stern and waited until everybody was quiet. "Nobody suspects senior citizens. They think we can't do anything. Well they're wrong."

"Damn right they're wrong!"

"They think we can't do anything. Now, can we?"

Mr. Glackens led the responses now. His pince-nez had fallen from his nose and was dangling from the front of his work shirt, but he seemed to see clearly without it. "Damn right we can."

A passerby looked their way with disapproval and then averted her eyes. She could have been passing a lunatic raving on a street corner, or stepping over a drunk.

Mr. Messer raised his hand. "When do we start?"

"When it's time."

"How will we know when it's time?"

"We'll know."

He sounded exasperated. "What do we do now?"

Victor said, "Right now, we wait. When it's time, we make them meet our demands."

Mr. Messer was too long-legged for the bench and he seemed irritated: at sitting, at not having anyplace to put his feet. "What are our demands?"

"We'll cross that bridge when we come to it," Victor said hastily. "You can be on the committee. Right now, we settle in and wait."

Settle in. Marian seized on the words with relief. She was tired from all the excitement and even Victor wasn't used to being on his feet for so long at a stretch. His speckled hands were jittering and there was a little muscle jumping in his cheek. She said, for all of them, "We should all take a load off our feet."

Sitting, Marian chattered with her bridge group; even Rebecca had warmed to the excitement and her eyes were sparkling prettily and her cheeks were pink. They shared a box of cookies Maud had intended for their next bridge meeting and on the whole it was as pleasant as any day they had passed at the senior center, or in the tea room at the Lady Eleanor Hotel. There was a rest room in the store opposite, and through the long day they went back and forth in shifts, making little purchases so they could ask for the rest room keys, which, finally, one of them managed to keep. The strain did not begin to tell until suppertime, when some people got cranky because they were used to having their main meal of the day at five, and others were querulous because they had missed their naps. Even Marian felt her energies flagging but she just ate a candy bar and freshened up with a Wash n' Dri. Two people picked up their belongings and left in a huff and three or four others drifted off to the rest rooms and simply drifted away. When Marian looked for Victor she saw him standing at the far end of the oval, in front of the little barricade of smoking stands. He had his back to them and all the angles of his body were cast in a mold of despair. She went to him.

"They weren't any of our people," she said. "They were only stragglers. We don't need their kind."

"Good girl." When he turned he was smiling too brightly. "Oh Marian I don't know whether I can bring this off."

"We've come this far. Of course you can."

"What can we do against them? Me, with my emphysema, all these other people with their bags of diseases. Walkers. Pacemakers. Hearing aids."

"There's nobody here with . . ."

"We can't make an army, we can't even make demands. What can we do? We're only a bunch of . . . senior citizens."

"And we are in the right," Marian said.

"Right doesn't make might."

"Maybe not, but it will make them pay attention. We deserve to be treated with respect."

"I was a fool to think we could manage this. Maybe we should all just . . ."

"You said it was do or die." If they gave up now and she had to go home to Sally and Albert and her empty bed and the soggy TV mix, it would be the end. She would just shrivel up and blow away and, she thought with a surprising flutter of the heart, so would Victor dry up and blow away. They had come this far and she was not going to let him turn back. "Do or die, remember? Now what's the point of dying, really?"

"That's it, of course. That's it."

"I bought something for you."

"What?"

"Something for tonight. T-shirts, you know, for uniforms? Maybe later we can get them to put on our names." She went on energetically, trying to rally them. "I got purple, would you rather have black?"

"Uniforms . . ."

"So people will know who we are and what we're doing."

"So they'll know what we're doing," he said slowly. "So—they'll —know—what—we're—doing!"

"Of course, if you'd rather have black . . ."

"Sit tight. I'm going to make a phone call." Something she had said had made him young.

"A phone call?"

"Insurance policy."

"Wait a minute, you haven't said which color you . . ." She shouted after him, "Be careful," but he went on as if he hadn't heard.

The showdown came at closing time, when security guards began flushing people out of the stores so owners could cover the counters and pull shut the metal grates. At the far end of the corridor the custodial staff was moving out with brooms and mops and waxers; Marian could hear them approaching from a long way off. Victor and his group would not be noticed right away because customers were still drifting out of stores, comparing purchases in the central plaza, where escalators and ramps fed into the circular path around the artificial plants that bordered the artificial fountain. The last teenagers were socking their remaining change into video games and kicking the machines, the last movies were just letting out and the last lost child was shuffling along in a droopy diaper, crying dismally. As the last shoppers departed the architect's design was revealed: the colonnades of shop-fronts, the expanses of terrazzo flooring, the vaulted glassed-in roof. Once the last bits of popcorn and matchbooks and crumpled paper napkins were swept away it would be almost idyllic, all those glossy surfaces enhanced by the fluorescent light. Far above their heads, a trapped bird flew.

Even the crankiest of Victor's people were quiet now, preternaturally alert. During the long evening they had gotten a second wind, nodding off when nobody was looking, easing out of tight shoes. At this hour most of them were wakeful anyway; at home they would be shaking off the effects of the after-dinner nap, girding for a night of insomnia. They would be sitting owlishly in front of the Late Show or calling up all-night radio programs to offer their opinions, routing grease out of the kitchen stove or simply rattling from window to window, waiting for the sun to come up so they could relax. Now all this energy was concentrated on the task at hand. Their ears were filled with the sound of their own blood rushing, the rattle of their dry breath. They would sit in silence in the bathtub-shaped rest area, fortified by the enormous patience that comes with age. They had waited much longer for less important things. What were the next few minutes, compared with the eternities that had already slipped by?

Regarding them, Marian was proud. In spite of the hardships of the day they were all sitting up straight with their hands folded, looking spunky and bright in their lightweight costumes, waiting for the last great adventure to begin. It did not matter what the risks were, what would be the cost; anything was better than the half-lives they were turning their backs on, the cramped existences in back bedrooms, retirement homes. Anything would be better than the logical end; to avoid it, they would do anything. She became aware that there was a watchman circling the rest area; on his third round he cleared his throat and her heart flopped like a stranded goldfish as he spoke.

"Excuse me."

Victor got to his feet, saying to his people: "This is it."

"I said, excuse me."

Victor said to Marian, "When it starts, watch me. Pass it on."

The watchman said, "I wonder if you folks would mind . . ."

Marian muttered, to Cecelia, "Victor says watch him. Pass it on."

As children they had all been taught never to speak to strangers and so nobody spoke. When he couldn't stand it any longer the night watchman rapped his nightstick against the Permastone. Several people jumped at the sound. "You have to go now, it's closing time."

Nobody spoke.

"You're going to have to leave. Are you all deaf?" He was shouting. *"I said, it's closing time."*

"We heard you," Victor said, and did not move. Some of the

women produced knitting, and Mr. Messer and Mr. Glackens resumed their cribbage game. Feeling more daring than she ever had, Marian brought out a length of dental floss and began a game of cat's cradle with Cecelia.

"Are you all crazy?"

"No," Victor said. "I don't think so. No."

During the long silence that followed somebody laid out a game of solitaire and two or three people pretended to snore. The watchman circled the rest area three times and then shrugged and left. When he returned it was with two others plus his supervisor, who was so important that he came to work in a business suit. The supervisor took a position just outside the barricade. "Who's in charge?"

Victor stood.

"LISTEN," the supervisor said slowly and in loud tones, in case they were all deaf. "YOU HAVE TO GO NOW. GO HOME. WE ARE CLOSING."

Victor did not respond.

"Do you speak English?"

"Of course I speak English, you damn fool."

"Then stop this. Give up. Go home. Do you hear me? *I said,* GO HOME."

"No thank you."

At a signal the watchmen raised their nightsticks.

"What are you going to do," Victor said in a tone that was meant to shame, "beat us to death?"

The supervisor grimaced. "No I'm not going to beat you to death. I'm going to call the police."

"Well go ahead."

The police, Marian thought with a shudder of embarrassment, but when she looked at Victor he was not embarrassed and neither was anybody else. Maybe this is like the sixties, here we are and here we'll stay, we will not be moved. When they arrived, the police huddled around the central fountain, while their sergeant approached alone. In a fit of excitement Marian began humming "We shall overcome," but Victor silenced her with a look.

The sergeant said, "What seems to be the trouble here?"

"No trouble, Officer."

"Oh, that's good." The sergeant blinked ingenuously.

"Everything is just the way I wanted it."

The sergeant said, patiently, "Do you know what time it is?"

"Half-past eleven, you idiot. Don't you have a watch?"

"Of course I do. I just wondered if you people knew, because if you did know, well, you'd know it was time you were all home in bed." He could have been addressing a group of five-year-olds. "Oh, but you can't get out. Somebody has put these great big smoking stands in your way."

"Don't touch those."

"Wait, and I'll get my men to move them."

Victor drew his gun. "Don't. Touch. Those."

The sergeant fell back a step.

Marian slid her hand into her pocketbook and closed it around the handle of Burton's straight razor. The others stirred, ready to arm themselves.

"Put that thing down."

"What if I don't?"

The sergeant put his hand on his own gun. "I'll give you ten seconds and then I draw. One . . ."

"What are you going to do, shoot me? Nice old man like me? What would the papers say?"

"Two . . ."

"Well if you want to, go ahead and shoot me, you'd be doing me a favor, my back is killing me."

"Three . . . Are you crazy?"

"And their backs are killing them," Victor said.

"Do you want to go to jail?"

"Oh hell, Officer, I don't care. None of us do."

Nonplussed, the sergeant looked past Victor, addressing Marian and the others. "Do you people want to go to jail?"

Victor turned. "OK, folks, what about it?"

At his signal Marian brought out Burton's razor and opened the blade. Next to her Cecelia brought out Shamus's old service revolver and the others brought out guns and bats and knives, whatever they had. Even the timid Rebecca was clenching her fists. Mr. Glackens had a Japanese sword.

"Like I said, Officer, we're all old here. Whatever we had was took from us, and as a result, we have nothing left to lose."

"All right," the sergeant said in a low voice, "what do you want?"

"We'll make a statement in the morning. Right now we want you to leave us alone."

"I can't do that and you know it."

"Leave us alone so we can get some rest. We're tired here."

"You know I can't. You know what I have to do."

Victor snorted. "Bring in the SWAT team, I suppose. Tear gas. Riot guns, the works. I'm warning you now. Just try it."

"This is your last chance to go quietly. This—"

At the far end of the corridor the outer doors crashed open to admit a huge man in a tuxedo, immediately followed by the press. A platoon of reporters, photographers, TV cameramen was heading down the empty hallway at full tilt. Victor's phone calls!

He had thought of everything.

As Victor rolled aside a smoking stand and headed out to meet the delegation, he managed a parting shot. "Do what you want, sonny, but it's going to be on the news."

The police stopped the press before they could reach the rest area, but Victor managed to shout a few words before a policeman halted him and forced him back.

"FREEDOM," he shouted for the microphones, waving his arms for the cameras. "GREY POWER." Marian was not sure what his last words were, but she thought they were, "TO ARMS."

She watched with a sinking heart as they pulled his arms behind him and marched him back to the rest area. All this trouble for nothing, she thought. All this grief. The police would send them all home and nobody would ever know. Nobody would find out even if it did get on the news because it was the middle of the night, when all decent people were asleep. Why wasn't Victor more upset? Why did he shake off the policemen and march the last few steps into the rest area with a triumphant grin? Did Victor know something they didn't know? She did not know. What she did know was that there was a persistent ringing sound; she waited for the rest—dizziness, the logical next thing after ringing in the ears, and when it did not come she realized that what she was hearing was the sound of a hundred different telephones in all the stores and all the offices in this great shopping center, all of them going at once.

After a lull the man in the tuxedo approached. He looked beaten, as if he knew the party he had been called away from would be over and forgotten before he settled this. "All right," he said wearily, "My name is Alexander Dawson, I'm the general manager. Now what do you people want?"

"We don't have any quarrel with you in particular," Victor said, "Thing is, this seems like as good a place as any to start."

As a first concession, Victor had him dim the overhead lights so he and his people could get some rest. Then he pointed out that the management had more to lose from this situation than he did, and Dawson agreed to unlock the nearest rest rooms so Victor and his people could make certain necessary trips. Then he withdrew so they could break out their collection of air mattresses and sleeping bags and settle down for the night.

Marian was far too excited to sleep. Lying on the terrazzo just outside the rest area, she imagined herself on any one of a hundred nights at the family cabin on the lake. When she was a little girl she and her cousins used to drag their mattresses outside so they could sleep under the midnight sky. It had been years since she had so much as seen a midnight sky and yet she could remember clearly everything she had felt: the excitement, the sense of being perpetually on the *verge,* the yearning for something she could not name. What had happened to her in the long years since that had left her frail and flatulent and near the end but still feeling all those same things? She was beyond the verge now, beyond almost everything but still filled with that same longing for something she could not identify. What had happened to her, that she never found it? What terrible accident had befallen her life? Even here in the middle of Florida, in this huge air-conditioned place with its polished surfaces, a thousand miles and several lifetimes away from the lake of her girlhood, she felt these same things. She could smell the night air and feel the earth on which she had slept. The scope of her losses puzzled her.

Maybe it was something I did.

She and Burton had honeymooned in that same cabin. The nights were like crystal, brittle with approaching autumn, and she lay in the big featherbed with Burton and knew that whatever it was she had wanted so much, this wasn't it. They went out in the mornings to look for berries but the season was already past. She wore her hair down like a little girl and by the time they left the lake she was pregnant with Sally, so that although her childhood had never ended, her long adulthood had begun. One day they put their things in the car and went back to town; the next day the light changed, and it was fall.

What was lost? What was it? She would have it or die. *Would,* she thought, starting out of what must have been a short sleep.

Victor would see to it.

Most of them were early risers—another of the functions of age— and so the camp was in good order long before the television crew returned. They were all ready for the day by 6 A.M.; Marian handed out the T-shirts on Victor's orders, and after a brief, rousing speech by Mr. Glackens, everybody put them on. It made an enormous difference to everybody's spirits to have them all there looking so spiffy, Marian thought with a little *frisson* of pride. She smiled and Victor smiled. They had all been to the rest room by this time, they were scrubbed and brushed and combed and feeling quite presentable after taking spit-baths in the sinks. They all breakfasted on supplies from the cache under the Permastone bench, breaking crullers with rising spirits; somebody made a joke and everybody laughed. By the time the first delegation of the morning arrived at the police barricade that had been set up between them and the outside doors, the senior citizens were looking smart and feeling good. They were ready for anything, or almost anything.

The police admitted the one group they had not expected to have to face. At a signal from Victor the childless among them armed themselves and fanned out to create a no-man's land where the cross and determined group of middle-aged children could meet for a parley with their delinquent parents.

Is that really my daughter? Marian wondered. *How did she get so old?*

At least Sally had combed her hair out of the rollers, but her housedress was frumpy and her face was a mess, starting with the expression of disapproval that exaggerated her wrinkles and bags. "Mother, aren't you ashamed of yourself?"

Marian eluded her clutch. "Don't try anything funny or my friends will fire."

"Good Lord, Mother, stop this foolishness and come home."

"By the way, have you killed any more roaches?"

"What?"

"The roach box. The *roach* box. I suppose it doesn't matter," she said with a sigh. It had crossed her mind that Victor might be wrong about the roach boxes, but it didn't matter because they needed to do this and any reason would do. "If it wasn't the roach boxes it would be something else."

"Have you gone crazy?"

"All you've ever wanted was to be rid of me. Well, you might as well know, I'm never coming home."

Sally's face was a study: ill-concealed relief, that Marian might not come back to sleep in the back bedroom and get in her way; embarrassment at having her mother involved in a public spectacle; resentment, Lord knew what else. "If you don't come out they're sending you to jail. They said this is your last chance."

"I don't think so."

"Mother, face it!"

"That's what I'm doing. Now will you go home?"

"Do you know what this will do to Albert's business? What am I going to say to all my friends?"

Next to them, Victor's son-in-law was hitting a similar note. "Haven't you caused enough trouble?"

"Think of the humiliation," Rebecca's daughter said.

Cecelia's nephew jerked her arm roughly. "First the pacemaker. Then the shoplifting. Now this."

"Sally, you look like hell in that housedress." Marian snapped open the razor. "Go home and do something to yourself."

Victor raised the pistol. "I'll show you trouble, if that's what you want."

Mr. Glackens nudged Cecelia's nephew with the tip of his speargun. He was short and round, but tough as nails. "I'd get out of here if I were you."

Sally's voice spiraled. "Mother, this is your last warning. If you don't come now they're going to take measures."

"Sez you." Deftly, Marian cut the tie to Sally's wraparound with Burton's razor. "If they want to take measures, let them," she said with a giddy laugh as Sally's wraparound swung open and her daughter gasped and pawed in a hasty attempt to cover herself. "Now are you going, or do we have to chase you out?"

The delegation of relatives withdrew in disorder, making heated statements to the incoming press. In the rest area Victor carefully explained the next phase. Mr. Glackens and Mr. Messer would guard the rest area while diversionary groups sauntered toward the police barricades—the one in the corridor and the one cutting them off from the central fountain. They would sidle over with kindly expressions, open foolish grins, just sweet old things out for a morning constitutional. They were armed and they had orders to stop anybody who tried to enter Victor's territory. Meanwhile Victor and the others took bolt cutters to the locks, opening the grates that protected the nearest stores. They opened a department store first and then a lunch stand and, in a fit of excitement, a pet shop, working quickly in the rising screech of a dozen different alarms. Then Marian and the others fanned out, scooping up supplies and, as instructed, doing a limited amount of damage—just enough to demonstrate their power. Marian's heart was fluttering in a tachycardic frenzy but she carried on, thrilled by the knowledge that for the first time since she could remember, she was making things *happen*. She and the others were doing something of great importance, and when they were finished everything would be changed.

The gambit brought not only the general manager in his rumpled tuxedo, but also the district manager, who had come from Atlanta in a helicopter, just to talk to them. Cecelia and two others ushered them in and they and Victor parleyed. They agreed to permit a 9 A.M. press conference, at which Victor would present his demands.

"Your children say you are all crazy and should be put away."

Victor brushed aside the microphone so he could look directly into the camera. "That's nothing. They've been trying to get rid of us for years."

"Mr. Wimsatt, do you have any proof?"

"You know as well as I do that everybody wants us dead."

There was a shocked silence in which the news people and camera crews all averted their eyes.

"Look at the way society treats us," Victor said with a bright smile. "You would think we all had leprosy, or something else they could catch."

The woman from Associated Press baited him. "Aren't you worried about what this will do to your children? The, ah, public embarrassment?"

"To hell with our children. We've been parents long enough."

The others took up the cry. "We've been parents long enough."

"Meanwhile I suppose you would like to know what are our demands." Victor had taken off his glasses for the press conference but when he unfolded the piece of paper he had taken from his pocket he pretended to be reading from it all the same. "Well, for one thing we want you to stop trying to get rid of us. Those ultrasound things, the sudden changes in medication, the skates at the top of the stairs . . ." He leaned into the microphone, cradling it confidentially. "I could tell you stories that would *curl your hair.*"

"Wait a minute, Mr. Wimsatt, are you alleging . . ."

"Look at it this way. We're all going to be gone soon enough."

He brushed aside the flurry of questions that followed with an impatient hand. "The second thing is . . . I said, *the second thing is,* we want a hundred thousand dollars in small bills. Maybe the city will kick in something but believe me, your storekeepers in this mall alone could make it up out of yesterday's receipts. You can put the money in an attaché case and send it in with your general manager, and if you do it right, you can still open your stores on time, right?"

Somebody in the embattled group began to hum and, carried away by the passion of the moment, Marian began to trill: "We shall overcome . . ."

Victor silenced them with an impatient hand. "The last thing we want is, we expect safe passage out of here and nobody to bother us afterward. No police chase, no recriminations, no charges of any kind. That means we want a municipal bus outside that exit and everybody cleared out of the mall and out of the parking lot and off the road leading away from here. Those are our demands."

"What if the city won't . . ."

"We'll hole up as long as we have to," Victor said.

"Are we to understand that you're prepared to make a last stand here?"

"We've come this far on our wits so I reckon we're ready to do whatever it takes."

If in her long sad life she had to make a last stand, Marian thought as they waited to see what would happen, she would like to make it here at the Ebb Tide Mall. She had been coming here ever since the place opened, from the time before Burton died to the sad day when the children decided she was too old to make it on her own and took her away from her house. Over the years she had brightened her own kitchen and decorated her person with tidbits purchased at the various shops; she had eaten at least a thousand ice cream cones in dozens of flavors, including ones that had been tried once by the ice cream chain and scratched off the list. She had cried in the back row during hundreds of movies in Cinemas One through Eight; she had let her hand trail in the central fountain until the joints ached and the tips of her fingers shriveled up. She had lost at least one ring in the sand in one of the planters and held hundreds of conversations with clerks in the various stores over products she had already forgotten, because she was grateful for the chance to hear herself talk. She had sampled snacks from ill-fated food stands with short seasons and eaten sushi and tried her teeth on bagels, strange fruit for an innocent from Waltham, Massachusetts, and she had walked more than a thousand miles on the gleaming terrazzo floors. Once she had even gone to the lawyers' kiosk in the west wing to contest a family will and she was fairly certain that although she had not located it, there was somewhere in the mall a funeral home with all the equipment necessary to deal with her last requests.

In a way, she thought, it might be better to die here than to have to face the world outside. If the bus was waiting for them and they all got on it, where were they going to go, and what would she do when they came to the end of the line? She had depended on others for so long that she was not sure she could still take care of herself. She went from her mother's house to Burton's to Sally's; what could she do, one woman alone, what could she do in the world? Looking at Maud and Cecelia and the others, all locked in their own meditative silences, she wondered whether they were worrying about some of the same things. Even Victor was silent. He was pacing outside the rest area with his head bent and his hands locked behind his back.

He looked like a general, preoccupied by intimations of the future, suffering the isolation of the leader, the loneliness that comes with command. Holding her breath, Marian slipped out of the rest area and as he described a quick turn and began pacing back in her direction, she approached him and spoke.

"Is something the matter?"

He looked at her with pale, empty eyes. "It might be better if they just wiped us out."

"What do you mean, better?"

"We all end the same place anyway. Why not get it over with?"

"Get it over with. Get it *over* with." She clutched her own collar and shook it in a rage. Somewhere inside, her heart seemed to be chasing its tail. "You got us all down here to get it over with?"

"Why now, I . . . ." He winced because she had punched him on the arm.

"You put us to all this trouble and made all this fuss?"

"I really believed we could do something, but now . . . ."

"Now they're out there doing what you say. What *you* say."

"I hope so."

"I know they are."

"Oh, Marian, maybe you're right. Oh, Marian . . . ."

"Why Mr. Wimsatt!"

"There's something I've been meaning to . . . My dear, if we get out of this . . . ."

"ALL RIGHT EVERYBODY, THIS IS THE MAYOR SPEAKING."

At the sound of the loudspeaker, they jumped apart. Victor's voice lifted. "This is it."

Everything went so smoothly that they should have been suspicious. The police barricades dissolved almost magically; as nearly as Marian could make out there was not even a watchman left in the mall. At the far end of the corridor the glass doors were opened to the hard, bright Florida sunlight. She could see the bus. The general manager brought the money in an attaché case and then stood by in a short, hostile silence while Victor counted it. They exchanged pieces of paper and the manager withdrew.

"It's all here."

Mr. Messer looked sepulchral, rather like a large stork that does not bring, but takes away. "What if it's marked?"

"Who are they going to arrest? This is a written entitlement. Now all we have to do is . . ." Victor looked into his hands and seemed to find them empty. "Well . . ."

There was no sound except for the hum of the air conditioning, the plash of the artificial fountain, which was punctuated now by rustling sounds: the chitter of old limbs shifting, dry skin rubbing dry fabric, partial plates snapping, the inexorable gurgle of trapped intestinal gas.

Victor said, "I guess this is it."

In that sad, lost moment, nobody spoke. Marian patted her hair and checked her makeup. She cleared her throat, wishing she had time to go to the rest room just once more because she was afraid of being caught short. She knew there was no time for that kind of thing and she clenched her teeth, hoping there would be a toilet on the bus. Touching Burton's razor, she brightened. The blade opened easily, the edge was sharp. Around her, the others were rearranging their clothes and checking their own weapons, patting thinning hair and sagging faces, trying on different expressions with which to meet the world and finding nothing appropriate. Marian reached into memory and brought forth the maternal frown that used to reduce the infant Sally to tears, laden as it was with the implied threat: *do that and I will murder you.*

Somebody, she thought it was Maud, began whistling through her teeth. She heard stocky, staunch Mr. Glackens humming nervously, and next to her, Cecelia, who could not stop snuffling, was trying fruitlessly to catch a postnasal drip. When she looked at Maud again, she was digging a nail between her two front teeth just exactly the way she had when she was a little girl, and they bought that wax candy at the corner store and chewed it together, sitting on the steps, and Marian saw that beneath the veil of years Maud's face was still wicked and funny, that same child's face. They were all having such a good time here, she thought, here in the safety of the mall. It was a pity they could not just spend the rest of their days in the air conditioning, trundling between the rest area and the shops. If the owner would only let them stay . . . but here was the satchel full of money, there were the open doors, and at the far end of the empty, sunlit expanse of asphalt stretching outside, the waiting bus . . .

"It's now or never." Victor would move them with his bare hands.

"Semper fi," said Mr. Glackens, who had been a Marine.

"Damn right," somebody said.

It was Mr. Messer who hit the right note. "Geronimo!"

"Geronimo!"

They began to move out.

"Remember, death before dishonor," Victor shouted.

If it was going to be death, Marian thought, would that be so much worse than the lives they left behind?

Mr. Glackens and Mr. Messer moved to either side of Victor, facing outward with their spearguns at the ready, the one looking like a compact little tank, invincible, and the other revolving with his elbows flapping, the picture of vulnerability. In one hand, Victor held the attaché case with the money; with the other he brandished the paper of entitlement like a magic talisman. Those who were armed made a ring around the others, who had picked up all the satchels, canvas totes, shopping bags and crumpled paper sacks that contained the necessaries, supplies, extra ammunition, underwear, along with the unnecessary: string collections, broken glasses, old photographs, the objects they had brought because they could not bear to leave home without. They made a solid phalanx, moving in Victor's wake.

Somebody began to sing.

It was not until they cleared the outer glass doors and started across the parking lot, a little muddled by the brilliant sunlight and blinking to protect their eyes, that the police revealed themselves. Suddenly there were huge helmeted figures slipping out from behind parked cars, motorcycles, anything large enough to conceal a man.

Oh no.

Victor was shouting, "It's a double cross."

"A double cross!" Mr. Glackens put himself directly in front of Victor to protect him, aiming his speargun in several directions at once.

"YOU HAVE THREE SECONDS TO PUT DOWN YOUR ARMS AND SURRENDER." It was the mayor. "ONE."

"Damn the torpedoes." Mr. Glackens was waving the speargun like a deranged Friar Tuck.

"TWO."

The little group kept moving. "Retreat hell," Mr. Messer cried, falling back so he protected Victor from the rear.

"THREE."

As Marian watched a policeman darted out of the advancing ranks and made a feint with a riot gun, and in the next second, in a whirl of activity so swift that it was hard to be sure who had done what, Mr. Glackens fired his speargun accidentally, piercing the hood of a Camaro he wasn't even aiming at. "You should be warned my hands are a legal weapon," Mr. Messer was screaming, and then everything else was obliterated by the shot.

The shot.

"NO," Victor shouted, whether to his ranks or to his enemy.

"No," Marian screamed, because she knew somebody was hurt but nobody had fallen. Victor? Who? She was weeping. "No."

A television camera had appeared from nowhere, recording everything as the mobile unit sent it out live to viewers in three counties. Later in the day the technicians would slow down the tapes for national broadcast, showing a horrified nation the scuba spear quivering in the Camaro's hood, and then in a series of freeze-frames poor Mr. Messer's anguished expression and Victor's grimace of despair as Mr. Glackens made a slow half-turn, gave his leader an apologetic look and fell. This all happened so fast, or was it so slowly, Marian wondered, so horribly that until he hit the asphalt and blood blossomed on the purple T-shirt, she did not even know he had been hurt.

"GO," the amplified voice shouted, and without regard for poor fallen Mr. Glackens or any of their feelings, the police began to converge on them, looking like giant insects in their silver helmets and their sunglasses; in another minute they would fall on the old people and break them in two and feed on their severed limbs.

"Oh please," Marian sobbed and put her face in her hands, thinking: *This is the end.* Was she relieved to have all her decisions taken from her? She could not be sure.

She hunched her shoulders, waiting with her eyes closed.

Victor was trying to get them to sing.

It was black behind her closed eyelids; soon she would feel a bullet or a crushing blow and give herself to complete blackness.

The end.

Nothing happened.

End.

Nothing at all.

Then as she crouched she heard a new sound, a roar or vibration that must have begun as Mr. Glackens fell, the steady and inexorable rumble of something huge awakening, the shuffle of a thousand feet, and when she opened her eyes, everything had changed.

They were still surrounded, all right, poor Mr. Glackens was still lying on the asphalt with the last light fading from his eyes, but there were only a few traces of police—one or two helmets rolling on the asphalt, and in the air the flash of shiny boots as police were tumbled over people's heads and coming from somewhere underfoot the cries of other policemen being trampled in the melee. What had happened, she realized as the mob surrounded them, was that Victor's last stand, the very possibility of change, had reached several thousand hearts. Victor had raised a great grey army, and now it was coming to their aid.

Their stand in the mall was the catalyst. It may have been a simple annoyance to the shopkeepers but for the senior citizens, it was a galvanizing event. It was like a war cry to the thousands of aging insomniacs who paced their houses in the wee hours, trying to pass the empty time by listening to the radio. The first bulletins had alerted them; whether he realized it or not, Victor's cries had brought them out. Now they were on the march. The restless, the superannuated, the aging and undesirable thousands had scribbled hasty notes for those they were leaving behind; they had put out extra food for the cats and overwatered their plants and then they had simply set their burglar lights on automatic timers and clicked their dead-bolt locks and walked into the night. Throughout the hours of darkness they had made their way across the city by car, by bus, by taxi, in motorized wheelchairs and on foot, filtering through the streets so quietly that nobody had even noticed until they materialized outside the mall at dawn. When the sun came up they were all standing there, with grim expressions becoming clear in the morning light.

Until the trouble started they simply made a ring around the vast parking lot, waiting quietly because over the years they had all learned how to wait. They were very careful to leave the driveways clear, and none of them strayed from the walks. They waited unchallenged because so far they were not doing anything and furthermore there was not a policeman alive who had the gall to challenge some old party who might have been a parent or grandparent. You could not poke your mother with a nightstick and tell her to move on.

Taken individually, the old people were not threatening. Their old hearts were jolted by pacemakers or helped by digitalis; many of them swayed on aluminum walkers or crutches or malacca sticks because they could not quite stand unsupported; there were the hard-of-hearing and the nearsighted and those whose blood pressure was kept at feasible levels by a battery of pills or whose digestive systems were stable only thanks to Lomotil; there were a bundle of artificial limbs and thousands of pairs of glasses and more than a few ostomy bags so that almost every member of Victor's army was technically augmented in some way. Taken individually, they would not have looked like much. En masse, they were invincible. They were, furthermore, heavily armed. They had come out with stout blackthorn sticks, cleavers and kitchen knives and machetes and gardening shears, with bats in tote bags and chains in paper sacks and a battery of rifles and sidearms, and now, having vanquished the police, they ringed Victor's little group, which they had delivered, and waited, breathing heavily, to find out what Victor's orders were.

Victor did not speak.

They had left a respectful little open space around Victor's group, separating the key members from the mob. Victor was the acknowledged leader and it was his place to order the next move. When he did not say anything the ring narrowed imperceptibly.

"Now what?" a bald man shouted from the front ranks. He was burly and conspicuous in a health-club T-shirt.

"What's next?"

"We want answers!"

Marian watched Victor with her heart fibrillating and her breath coming in sobs. What could he tell them? What on earth were they going to do? This was more than she had asked for and she thought it was more than Victor had asked for too. The circle was tightening.

"Speech." It was an entreaty.

"Speech." It was a threat.

It was an order. Six burly men were converging on them. They were all wearing health-club T-shirts, which seemed to be red. They picked Victor up and moved him through the crowd to the mayor's Lincoln, which had been abandoned in the rout and before anybody could stop them they set him on the roof. "Speech."

Victor cleared his throat. His voice was faint. "I'd like to thank you all for coming here."

"Louder!"

"I said, THANK YOU." He was so obviously shaken by all this that Marian was afraid. Somebody must have decided she was a person of importance; she and all the other members of Victor's group were brought forward so that she was close enough to touch the mayor's chromium hood ornament. "We got the money, which I would be more than happy to share with you."

The murmur of disappointment was frightening.

Victor raised his hands for silence. "And we got their attention. They don't dare to try and hurt us now." He looked directly into the television camera, which was in the hands of one of their number and still operating. "You don't dare try and hurt us now."

"More!"

"So you see, we've won."

The murmur of disappointment became a rumble.

A young sprat in his late sixties had taken a position on the hood of the Lincoln. He was wearing one of those health-club T-shirts and his muscles bulged. He looked at Victor, posing questions for the crowd. "What do we do next?"

"Maybe we've done enough."

"Never!"

A woman wailed. "We can't just go home."

"What do we do next?"

"Have a war council?" Victor looked unsure.

Marian and Mr. Messer and several others took up the cry. "War council."

"War council." Cecelia.

"War council." Rebecca! This thing had been good for her.

"To hell with that," Victor's adversary cried. "On to City Hall."

The man in the health-club T-shirt was joined by his henchmen; they lifted the unwilling Victor from the car and raised him on their shoulders. "On to City Hall."

"Wait," he shouted. "Please wait."

"On to City Hall."

Marian did not need to worry about keeping track of Victor; she and the others had been picked up and carried high on the shoulders of the mob. They were being borne along like ceremonial objects, the living standards of the revolution, whose function was to inspire the crowd in what had become a holy mission. If the old people were inspirited by news of the stand in the mall, the death of Mr. Glackens had set them wild. One trio had picked up Mr. Messer and were waving him like an unsightly flag. Another group handled Maud like a medicine ball.

"Wait," Marian said as she was raised aloft, and she heard Mr. Messer and some others begging their supporters to wait.

Victor bobbed along in the vanguard, shouting, "Stop it, please! This is not what I intended."

It was too late.

By this time Marian was being carried along next to Victor and she may have been the only one who heard him wail, "All I ever wanted was to get it back."

Where were the police? When Mr. Glackens fell, he accomplished more than he would ever know. He had saved Victor's life by giving his own and started this great army moving but there was more. He had neutralized the police. How could they attack these nice old people when every detail would go out over the air? How could they level guns at other people's grandparents as the nation watched? The switchboard at headquarters was already jammed with angry calls. An order came out of the mayor's office for them to avoid confrontation. Riding on the crest of the human tidal wave, Marian would realize that the mob was beyond confrontation now, beyond human interference, it moved like an inexorable natural force.

The air was made hideous by guttural cries and sickening crashes as the mob limped and shuffled out of the parking lot, attacking and stripping motorcycles, overturning cars. The progress to City Hall was slow but as devastating as a lava flow or a firestorm that feeds on itself, gaining in power as it goes. The crowd had filled the streets, stopping all traffic and spilling into private property, swelling as it flowed. At every point the mob was augmented by outraged seniors who tore out of their houses in full cry, ready to go to war. By nightfall there would be several collapses from stroke or heart attack or simple heat exhaustion but these were the fresh morning hours, the adrenaline was racing through all those old veins, these good people were together in something for the first time, just beginning to realize their strength. Their energy was high. In less than an hour all these senior citizens had been catapulted from the hopelessness of waning lives into a growing power, discovering that power begets power; they were delirious with it and they swept along like a firestorm that feeds on itself and, feeding, moves on. The old people routed householders and shopowners and stray pedestrians, who hastily took cover. Unchallenged, they moved on, trampling gardens and crunching hedges, leveling small trees, toppling bird baths and garden statues and street signs and anything else that got in the way, smashing windows and shattering plate glass as they went, looting, pillaging, destroying everything in their path. The few homeowners who had stayed behind to defend their property were quite simply crowded out by the aged legions. Nothing stood for long in their path. They were decent people who had endured lifetimes of illness and hardships and terrible events and tried to keep smiling, enduring infirmities and insults with good cheer, only to be put out to pasture, shunned and despised, relegated to the back rooms and garbage heaps of a society that wanted nothing more than to do away with them.

Now their moment had come. Venerable as they were, whitehaired or potato bald, scored by wrinkles and bent with arthritis and raddled by osteomyelitis and cancer of a dozen different kinds, kept alive by a veritable pharmacy, they were on the march and they were ready to keep marching until they got what they wanted or died.

If they could not be young again then they wanted to be honored, perhaps even feared.

They wanted to be treated with respect.

The sun was on the wane by the time they reached City Hall. Throughout the long march foraging parties had fanned out into supermarkets and specialty shops to keep the marchers supplied with food and drink, and nobody asked where or how they all managed to relieve their bladders, and as they grew tired from being on their feet for so many hours at a stretch, nobody asked where or how they were going to sleep.

The mayor had erected a small platform with bunting and loudspeakers on the front steps of City Hall, and as the front ranks arrived and eddied at the bottom of the steps, he began to speak.

"THERE YOU ARE," he said from his vantage point at the top of the long flight of granite steps. As the crowd set Marian and Victor and the others down and they tried their legs he went on. "NOW AREN'T YOU ASHAMED?"

Supported by one of the burly health-club members, Victor made his way up the steps and as he climbed, the crowd cheered and applauded and somebody raised the cry: "Freedom now."

"No we are not ashamed," Victor began, but the mayor was holding the microphone out of his reach.

"NOW I WANT YOU TO PUT DOWN YOUR ARMS AND GO HOME." The mayor's aside to Victor was also picked up and amplified. "Tell them to put down their arms and go home."

She saw Victor shake his head.

"IF YOU GO HOME NOW THERE WILL BE NO REPRISALS," the mayor said, and again the speakers carried his aside. "Tell them if they go now there will be no reprisals."

"Hell no!"

Even though Victor was off mike the mob heard and took up the cry. "Hell no."

"IF YOU DON'T GO NOW WE ARE GOING TO HAVE TO FIND A SOLUTION," the mayor said. "THIS IS YOUR MAYOR SPEAKING, AND I KNOW WHEREOF I SPEAK."

Victor was panting from the effort to be heard without the microphone. "What kind of solution?"

"SOMETHING FINAL," the mayor said and then dropped the mike in horror because he was on the air, and blaring out of every speaker.

Victor picked it up. "DIDN'T I TELL YOU?"

Behind the multiple glass doors leading out of City Hall dark shadows moved.

"I TOLD YOU THEY WERE TRYING TO GET US."

Marian realized the dark shapes were armed police. "Look out!"

Victor turned to the mayor. "SMILE, YOU'RE ON TV," he said, and it was true. He and the others were both observed and protected by the presence of the media; they both knew it. The mayor raised his hand and the shadows behind the glass doors stopped moving and withdrew.

"LET US REASON TOGETHER," Victor began.

Somebody cried out: "NO."

A hundred other voices cried, "NO!"

"WE HAVE TO REASON." Victor had to shout to be heard. "WE HAVE TO TALK . . ."

There was an outraged shriek. "Talk!"

"We want action."

"PLEASE!" An arm hooked around Victor's throat and cut him off. A dozen health-clubbers in red T-shirts swarmed up the steps and the bald man who had caused so much trouble seized the microphone as the others overpowered the mayor and in a frenzy dragged him down the steps. The crowd parted like a human sea. There were already cries of "String him up." Someone produced a rope and they lashed the captive mayor to the huge bronze knees of the statue of Lincoln that adorned the plaza in front of City Hall. Marian could see Victor tugging at the T-shirt of the man who usurped the microphone, but the militant brushed him off as casually as he would a fly and then his minions dragged poor Victor down the steps and deposited him, gasping, at Marian's feet. The coup was complete.

The new voice boomed over their heads and bounced off the buildings surrounding the plaza. Its owner looked like Mr. Glackens gone awry: similar in stature but contorted by the urge to kill. "MY NAME IS VANCE BIGGERS, AND THIS IS WAR."

That night the old people warmed themselves at a hundred different campfires while the mayor writhed and tugged at his bonds and protested and finally fell silent, as police cruisers circled the area and police helicopters chattered overhead. It was only a matter of time before somebody brought in the army; Marian knew it and the others knew it too. Her heart was faltering and her old joints were seizing up in the gathering chill.

She started at the sudden warmth that suffused her as Victor slipped his arm around her waist.

"We've come a long way from what we wanted."

She sighed. "How did it happen so fast?"

He shrugged and shook his head.

They leaned close for comfort and for a long time neither of them spoke. They were afraid of what would happen in the morning and they had both cooled fast in the gathering shadows, fully aware that it was getting late and they were afraid. Looking around in the sullen glow of a hundred smoky fires, Marian wondered how many others were afraid.

Vance Biggers, the new leader, had refused to parley with Victor or any of his people. He had refused to parley with the governor. He had refused to parley at all. He called a press conference to announce his intentions, so Marian and Victor and the grey army and discomfited state officials and the rest of the world all heard about them all at once. What he and the mob wanted, he said, were three things. His voice was the voice of a man drunk on his own success, and the vicious singsong reminded Marian of certain other leaders, and the misery they had caused. What they all wanted, he said, was financial restitution for all the losses imposed by mandatory retirement, plus a little for the insult. They wanted guarantee of safe conduct and the establishment of a separate, free state, with enough money thrown in to make it a luxury haven for the old.

In his own press conference, the governor set a deadline for the safe return of the mayor and warned the old people they had gone one step too far. His second deadline was for their surrender. They had twelve hours to disperse peacefully before the police moved in, followed by local units of the National Guard. He would call on federal troops if he had to, to finish the job.

At his 11 P.M. press conference Vance Biggers announced that he and his were ready to fight to the death.

So there it was.

Or was it, Marian wondered, nearer to tears than she had been for a long time. As the fires dwindled and the night grew deeper, she had the sense that the group was diminishing. There were simply not as many of them here. The man who had been roasting hot dogs at the next campfire was gone and Mr. Messer was gone from their own circle and she hadn't seen Maud in hours. Had those people seen what was coming and slipped away? How many others were slipping away? She shuddered to think about the morning: the suffering, the loss, and she shuddered to think about the carnage their mob had caused. Half the city was in ruins; any bridges she might have had left, she had burned, and she could not imagine how this could end anywhere but in jail, or in the grave. Would she have to go to jail? If she did, she hoped she and Victor would be near enough to each other to visit, perhaps on Sundays in the prison yard, or on movie nights, or with a special pass. Her chin was trembling. Even that, she realized, would be better than the grave. If she started crying now she would just keep on crying until all the parts of her just softened up and washed away. She reached for Victor's hand.

"Oh Marian, how did two nice old folks like us get mixed up in a thing like this?"

"This is not your fault, Victor." She felt his fingers tighten on hers and she squeezed back. "It's none of it your fault."

Then without exchanging a word they both stood up at the exact same moment, quivering in the dark. It would be hard to slip away without being stopped by one of the extremists, but the crowd was still thick enough to make it possible. They had no time to lose. Vance Biggers and the others were so drunk on their triumph that they had not yet noticed that their crowd was dwindling. This left only the police to prevent them from leaving, Marian thought, and then she realized that the police probably wanted them to go. Very well, she thought, as she and Victor cleared the last clump of senior citizens and tiptoed over the last trampled ornamental border and began to sprint across the street. They would simply disappear.

Victor had turned over the money in the attaché case to the new central committee, but she knew he had put his savings in traveler's checks and she had her savings in traveler's checks. It was not much for a beginning, but it would have to do.

She whispered, to Victor, "Do you really think they were trying to kill us with the roach boxes?"

"I don't know, but if they were, they won't try it again."

In spite of the hour, her fatigue, the unknown she had just stepped into, Marian gave a little skip. She and Victor would go someplace new and start over. What more could a nice old couple want?

The Bride of Bigfoot

Imagine the two of us together, the sound of our flesh colliding; the smell of him. The smell of me.

At first I was afraid. Who would not be frightened by stirring shadows, leaves that shiver inexplicably, the suspicion that just outside the circle of bug lamps and firelight something huge has passed? If there was a Thing at all it was reported to be shy; the best photographs are blurred and of questionable origin; hunters said it would not attack even if provoked, but still . . . The silence it left behind was enormous; I could feel my heart shudder in my chest. With gross figures roaming, who would not be afraid?

We did not see or hear it; there was only the intimation. It had been there. It was gone. Thomas, whom I married six months ago, said, Listen. I said, I don't hear anything. Roberta said, I'm cold. Thomas persisted: I thought I heard something. Did you hear anything? I did not speak but Malcolm, who was torturing steaks on our behalf, spoke politely. Everybody's so quiet, it must be twenty of or twenty after. Then Roberta said, Something just walked over my grave. I tried to laugh, but I was cold.

This was the night of our first cookout of the summer, shortly before I found certain pieces of my underwear missing from the line.

Our house is on the outer ring of streets here, so that instead of our neighbors' carports and arrangements for eating outside we look out at a wooded hillside, dense undergrowth and slender trees marching up the slope.

If it weren't for dust and attrition and human failure our house would be picture perfect. I used to want to go to live in one of our arrangements; the future would find me among the plant stands, splayfooted and supporting a begonia; I would be both beautiful and functional, a true work of art. Or I would be discovered on the sofa among the pillows, my permanent face fixed in a perpetual smile. I would face the future with no worries and no obligations, just one more pretty, blameless thing. It's a long road that knows no turning but an even longer one we women go. Each night even as I surveyed my creation I could see fresh dust settling on my polished surfaces, crumbs collecting on my kitchen floor, and I knew soon the light would change and leaves drop from my plants no matter what I did. Each night I knew I had to turn from my creations and start dinner because although Thomas and I both worked, it was I who must prepare the food. Because women are free and we are in the new society I was not forced to do these things; I had to do them by choice.

But it was summer, we opened all the windows and went in the yard without coats. We had that first cookout and maybe it was the curling smoke that wakened it, or maybe it saw me in my bathing suit . . . All I can tell you is that I lost certain underthings: my satin panties, my gossamer sheen bra. When I came home from work at night I went directly into the back yard. I tried to penetrate the woods, staring at the screen of leaves for so long that I was certain I had seen something move. The summer air was already dense with its scent, but what it was I did not know; I could not be sure whether that was a tuft of hair caught in the wild honeysuckle or only fur. Every night I lingered and therefore had to apologize to Thomas because dinner was late.

Something dragged a flowering bush to our back stoop. Outside our bedroom the flowers were flattened mysteriously. I got up at dawn and listened to the woods. Did I imagine the sound of soft breath? Did I catch a flash of gold among the leaves, the pattern of shadows dappling a naked flank?

In midsummer something left a dead bird with some flowers on my kitchen table and I stopped going outside. I stopped leaving the windows open, too; I told Thomas we would sleep better with the air conditioning. I should have known none of our arrangements are permanent. Even with the house sealed and the air conditioner whirring I could hear something crashing in the woods. I ran to the back door to see and when I found nothing I stood a moment longer so that even though I could not see it, it would see me. When we went to bed that night it was not Thomas I imagined next to me, but something else.

In August I retreated to the kitchen; with the oven fan going and the radio on, the blender whizzing and all my whisks and ladles and spatulas laid out I could pretend there was nothing funny happening. We had seafood soufflé one night and the next we had veal medallions, one of my best efforts. When we went to bed Thomas turned to me and I tried to be attentive but I was already torn. I was as uneasy as a girl waiting for somebody new to come to the high school party —one of those strange, tough boys that shows up unexpectedly, with the black T-shirt and the long, slick hair, who stands there with his pelvis on the slant and the slightly dangerous look that lets you know your mother would never approve.

On Friday I made salmon mayonnaise, which I decorated with cress and dill, and for dessert I made a raspberry fool, after which I put on my lavender shift and opened the back door. In spite of the heat I stood there until Thomas came in the front door. Then I touched the corners of the mats and napkins on my pretty table and aligned the wineglasses and the water tumblers because Thomas and I had pretty arrangements and we set store by them.

Honey, why such a big kiss?

I missed you, I said. How was your day?

Much the same.

So we sat down at the little table with all our precious objects: the crystal candle holders, the wedding china, the Waterford, him, me. I asked if he liked his dinner.

Mmmm.

All right; I tried to slip it in. Am I doing something wrong?

I'm just a little tired.

Tell me about your day, you never do.

Mmm.

Outside, the thing in the woods was stirring. Thomas, love is to man a thing apart, it's woman's whole existence.

Mmmmm.

In the woods there was the thunder of air curdling: something stopping in mid-rush.

I love you, Thomas.

I love you.

Honey, are you sure?

Mmmmm.

I put out a dish of milk for it.

No, Lieutenant, there were no signs of a struggle, one reason I
didn't think to call you right away. I thought she had just stepped
out and was coming back. When I got home from work Monday she
was gone. Nothing out of order, nothing to raise your suspicions, no
broken windows or torn screens. The house was shining clean. She
had even left a chicken pie for me. But there was this strange, wild
stink in the bedroom, plus which later I found *this* stuck in the
ornamental palm tree on our screen door, your lab could tell if it's
hair, or fur.

I wish I could give you more details, like whether the thing
knocked my wife out or tied her up or what, but I wasn't too careful
looking for clues because I didn't even know there was a Thing. For
all I knew she had run over to a neighbor's, or down to the store to
pick up some wine, which is what I thought in spite of the heap of
clothes by the bed, thought even after it got dark.

By midnight when I hadn't heard I called her folks. You can
imagine. Then I checked the closet with my heart going, clunk,
clunk. Nothing gone. Her bankbook and wallet were in her purse.
All right, I should have called you but to tell the truth I thought it
was something I could handle by myself. Ought to handle. A man
has a right to protect what's his, *droit de seigneur,* OK? Besides, I
didn't think it was kidnappers. That grey fur. The smell. It had to be
some kind of wild animal, an element with which I am equipped to
cope. I used to hunt with my father, and I know what animals do
when they're spooked. Your cordon of men or police helicopter could
panic it into doing something we would all be sorry for. I figured if it
was a bear or wolf or something that got in, and it didn't kill her
right here, it had probably carried her off to its lair, which meant it
was a job for one man alone. Now I have my share of trophies, you
might as well know back home I was an Eagle Scout and furthermore I am a paid-up member of the N.R.A. Plus which, this is not
exactly the wilds. This is suburban living enhanced by proximity to
the woods. If something carried off my wife I would stalk it to its lair

and lie in wait. Then when it fell asleep or went off hunting, I would swarm in and carry her out.

All right, it did cross my mind that we might get an exclusive. Also it was marginally possible that if I rescued her we might lure the creature into the open. I could booby-trap the terrace and snare it on the hoof. Right, I had guessed what it was, imagine the publicity! The North American serial rights alone . . . After which we could take our sweet time deciding which publisher, holding the paperback auction, choosing between the major motion picture and an exclusive on TV. I personally would opt for the movie, we could sell backward to television and follow up with a series pilot and spinoff, the possibilities are astronomical, and if we could get the thing to agree to star . . .

But my Sue is a sentimental girl and I couldn't spring this on her all at once. First I had to get her home and then I was going to have to walk her through it, one step at a time, how I was going to make it clear to the public that she was an unwilling prisoner, so nobody would think she was easy, or cheap. You know how girls are. I was going to have to promise not to take advantage of her privileged relationship with the Thing. But what if we could train it to do what we wanted? What if we taught it to talk! I was going to lay it out to her in terms of fitting recompense. I mean, there is no point being a victim when you can cash in on a slice of your life.

Lord, if that was all I had to worry about! But what did I know? That was in another country, and besides . . . Right, T. S. Eliot. I don't want you to think of me as an uncultivated man.

I got up before dawn and dressed for the hunt: long-sleeved shirt and long trousers, against the insects; boots, against the snakes. I tied up my head for personal reasons and smeared insect repellent on my hands and face. Then I got the rest of my equipment: hunting knife, with sheath; a pint of rye, to lure it; tape recorder, don't ask; my rifle, in case. A coil of rope.

It took less time to track it than I thought. You might not even know there was anything in the woods because you're not attuned to these things, but I can tell you they left a trail a mile wide. Broken twigs, twisted leaves, that kind of thing. So I closed in on their arrangement while it was still light; I came over the last rise and down into a thicket and there it was. I had expected to have a hard time locating her once I got to the lair; the Thing would have tied her in a tree, say, or concealed her under a mass of brush or behind a pile of rocks.

This was not the case. She was right out in the open, sitting on a ledge in front of its lair just as nice as you please. Except for the one thing, you would think she was sunning in the park. Right. Except for the dirt and the flowers in her hair, she was *au naturel.* There was my wife Susie sitting with a pile of fruits in season, she was not tied up and she was not screaming, she wasn't even writing a note. She was—good Lord, she was combing her hair. I went to earth. I had to be careful in case the Thing was using her for bait. It could be in its cave lying in wait, or circling behind me, ready to attack. I lay still for an hour while she combed and hummed and nothing happened. There was nothing, not even a trace. I got up and showed myself.

I guess I startled her. She jumped three feet. I said, Don't be frightened, it's me.

Oh, it's you. Where did you come from?

Never mind that now. We have to hurry.

What are you doing?

Suze, I have come to take you home.

Imagine my surprise. All this way to rescue my darling helpmate, the equipment, precautions, and all she could find to say was: You can't do that.

What do you mean?

So she was trying to spare my feelings, but that would take me some time to figure out. You have to go for your own good, Thomas. He'll tear you limb from limb.

Just let him try. I shook my rifle.

Thomas, no!

I did not like the way this was going. Not only was she not thrilled to see me but she showed signs of wanting to stay put. I was not sure what we had here, whether she was playing a game I had not learned the rules to or whether she had been unhinged by the experience. You should only have to court a woman once. What I did at this point was assert my rights. Any husband would have done the same. I said, Enough is enough, honey, now let's get home before it gets dark. Listen, this is for your own good. Susie, what are you doing with that rock?

To make a long story short I had to bop her on the head and drag her out.

I don't know how we made it back to the house. Halfway down the hill she woke up and started struggling so I had to throw her on the ground and tie her up, in addition to which the woods were filled with what I would have to call intimations of the creature. There was always your getting pounced upon from the shadows, or jumped out of a tree onto, to say nothing of your getting grabbed from behind and shaken, your neck snapped with one pop. I kept thinking I heard the Thing sneaking up behind me, I imagined its foul breath on my neck. As a matter of fact I never saw hide nor hair of it, and it crossed my mind that there might never have been a Thing, a thought I quickly banished. Of course there had. Then I figured out that it was afraid to run after what it believed in, which meant that it was craven indeed, to let her go without a fight.

As soon as we got inside I locked all the doors and windows and put Susie in the tub with a hooker of gin and a pint of bubble bath, after which, together, we washed all that stuff out of her hair, including the smell. I guess the gin opened the floodgates; she just sat there with the tears running down her cheeks while I picked the flowers out of her hair. Somehow I knew this was not the time to bring up the major motion picture. What we had here might turn out to be private and not interesting to anybody but us.

There there, Suze, I said. Don't feel bad.

She only cried louder.

Now we know who loves you the most.

She just kept on crying.

I tried to cheer her up by making a joke. Maybe it found a cheap date.

She howled and wouldn't speak to me.

So I looked at her naked, heaving shoulders and I thought: *Aren't you going to apologize?* I was afraid to ask but I had to say something; after all, she was my wife.

Don't be ashamed, Suze. We all get carried away at least once in our life.

When she would not stop crying I thought it must have been one of those one-night stands, if the thing cared about her at all it would be tearing the house down to get to her. She would get over it, I thought. But she would not be consoled. There there, I said, there there. When this blows over I'll buy you a car.

Fat lot I knew. It was a tactic. All the Thing had to do was *lay* back and wait for her to get loose. Which I discovered shortly before dawn when I woke to an unusual sound. I sat up and saw her moving among the bedroom curtains, trying to unlock the sliding door. Was the thing in the bushes, waiting? Would she run outside with cries of delight? I was afraid to find out. I sprang up and tackled her, after which I laid down the law. She didn't argue, she only wept and languished. It was terrible. I had tried to arm against the enemy outside and all the time I had this enemy within. I called us both in sick at work after which I marched her with me to the hardware store and surveilled her the whole time I was buying locks. Then I barred the doors and put extra locks on all the windows. The Thing was so smart it wasn't going to show itself. It was just going to sit tight and wait. Well two could play at that game, I thought. When it got tired of waiting and showed itself I would blow it apart.

I suppose I was counting too much on her. I thought sooner or later she would clean herself up and apologize and we could go back to our life. Not so. We went from vacation time into leave without pay and she was still a mess. She would not stop crying and she wouldn't speak to me. She just kept plastering herself to the windows with this awful look of hope. In addition to which, there was the smell. In spite of everything we still had this strange and fearsome smell. It would fill the room when I least expected it. My Susie would lift her head and sniff and grin and if I tried to lay a hand on her, look out! It was enough to make a grown man weep.

I had to act.

So what I did was put her in the cellar and lock her up, after which I put on my hunting clothes and located the equipment: rifle, knife, rope. The tape recorder, she had smashed. I didn't know how far I would have to stalk the Thing or what I would have to do to make it show itself but I was sick of the waiting game. Damn right I was scared. I took the double bar off the back door and went down the steps.

I tiptoed across the night garden, and over to the trees. I know you're in there, I said in a reasonable tone. If you don't come out I'm coming in after you.

There was nothing, only the smell. I thought I would pass out.

Homewrecker. Bastard, come on. Right, I was getting mad. I cocked the rifle. In another minute I was going to spray the trees.

Then it showed itself. It just parted the maples like swinging doors and walked out.

Huge. Yes, and that fetor, wow! The hair that covered it, the teeth . . . You've heard tales brought back by hunters. You can imagine the rest. The Thing stood there in the moonlight with its yellow teeth bared while I kept my rifle trained on its chest. It just stood there snuffling. I was, all right, I was overconfident. I yelled: Are you going to leave Susie and me alone or what?

At which point it sprang. Before I could even squeeze the trigger this great big monstrous thing sprang right on top of me after which I don't remember much except the explosion of my rifle, the kick. So it must be wounded, at least, which I suppose means it has left a trail of blood, but Lieutenant, I don't want to press charges. The thing is my Susie left me of her own free will and now that all is said and done I understand.

No I can't explain, not exactly, except it has to do with the Thing: the stench, the roar, the smack of its prodigious flesh. It must have squeezed the daylights out of me and thrown me into Malcolm's grape arbor, which is where I woke up. They were gone and he was calling the police.

I'm letting her go, Lieutenant, and with my blessings, because I learned something extraordinary in that terrible embrace. There are things we don't *want* to want but that doesn't stop us wanting them, even as we beg forgiveness. Life lets us know there is more than the orderly lines we lay out, that these lines can flex so we catch glimpses of the rest, and if a thing like this can happen to my Susie, who am I to say what I would do if it happened to me?

Hubbies: A Note

The hubbies frolic in the morning sunlight with their children; it is a treat to see them with their strollers and their catcher's mitts, heading for the park.

What do they talk about when they put their heads together? What race memory stirs and makes them yearn for something they cannot identify, something they know is lost?

They say that in the old days hubbies ran wild, eating and drinking, sleeping where they fell. In those times people stayed out of their way because the wild hubbies ran in packs and took their pleasure where they found it. Often a pack of wild hubbies would terrorize an entire countryside for days, wreaking havoc beyond history's powers of recording.

Most people would find that hard to believe, looking at the hubby of today. He is friendly and gentle, with his hair thinning and his feet grown pink and soft from centuries of domestication.

When she leaves in the morning the hubby will go to the window with a sigh. What thoughts pass through his head as he watches her out of sight? What memories stir him? How will he occupy himself until her return, and when he greets her with a deep sigh is it relief he is expressing, because she is home and safe, or is it unacknowledged rage?